The Big Hello

Books by Michael Lister

(John Jordan Novels)
Power in the Blood
Blood of the Lamb
Flesh and Blood
The Body and the Blood
Blood Sacrifice
Rivers to Blood

(Short Story Collections)
North Florida Noir
Florida Heat Wave
Delta Blues
Another Quiet Night in Desparation

(Remington James novels)
Double Exposure
Separation Anxiety

(Merrick McKnight novels)
Thunder Beach
A Certain Retribution

(Jimmy "Soldier" Riley novels)
The Big Goodbye
The Big Beyond
The Big Hello

(Sam Michaels and Daniel Davis Series)
Burnt Offerings
Separation Anxiety

The Big Hello
Michael Lister

a novel

PULPWOOD PRESS

Panama City, FL

Inquiries should be addressed to:
Pulpwood Press
P.O. Box 35038
Panama City, FL 32412

Lister, Michael.
The Big Hello / Michael
Lister.
-----1st ed.
p.   cm.
ISBN: 978-1888146-41-7 (hardback)
ISBN: 978-1-888146-42-4 (trade paperback)

Library of Congress Control Number:

Book Design by Adam Ake

Printed in the United States

1 3 5 7 9 10 8 6 4 2

First Edition

For Jason Hedden
collaborator, friend, brother

Thank you

Dawn, Jill, Adam, Travis,
Aaron, Jason, Allen

Chapter 1

Night was falling fast.

Clip and I were driving east toward Tallahassee, the final flare of fading sunburst burning out behind the pines lining the horizon behind us.

The descending darkness blanketing the earth seemed to be settling in, as if for a long black night—the kind where bad people operate with impunity, and in which bad things happen. Dark deeds that, like death, can't be undone.

Though one-armed and injured, I was driving—and not just because Clip couldn't see for shit at night with his one eye, but because he didn't want to be mistaken for my chauffeur.

We were searching for Lauren Lewis—something I had been doing my entire life.

Earlier in the day, weak, weary, and without sleep, we had stood alongside Henry Folsom, the best cop I knew and my old boss, over an open wound in the earth that was supposed to be Lauren's grave.

Headstone and hard dirt removed, coffin raised to reveal she wasn't inside.

Now, once again, I was in search of her, bumbling around in the dark trying to find her.

Her bent banker husband's final words still haunted me, echoing like the demented taunts of a madman in the claustrophobic chamber that was my mind.

Spoken the moment after I slit his throat, his life spilling out of him onto the floor, he had harshly whispered with the voice of death, " . . . was going to tell you just . . . before you . . . died. Guess . . . will be before . . . I do . . . Lauren's alive . . . I had her declared . . . DOA . . . took her far . . . far away . . . got her . . . best care possible . . . nursed her back . . . Wanted you . . . both to know . . . I knew . . . wanted you to suffer . . . to be tortured and . . . die horrible deaths . . . she will. No one knows who she is . . . you will . . . never find . . . her. I mean . . . never. You . . . helped kill her . . . again . . . you just . . . killed the only person . . . on the planet . . . who knows . . . who and . . . where . . . she—

As if knowing what I was thinking, Clip said, "Just 'cause Harry say she alive don't mean she is."

I didn't say anything.

He had his eye patch off and the mangled scar of socket was jarring.

"Just 'cause she not the one in that box don't mean she not in some box somewhere," he continued. "Know you ain't wantin' to hear it. Hell, I ain't wantin' to be sayin' it, but . . ."

He was right and I knew it.

I glanced over at him, at the narrow boniness inside the too loose suit.

"Then why you keep sayin' it?" I asked.

"'Cause you needs to hear it," he said.

I shook my head.

"You gots to prepare for—"

"Already lost her twice. That hasn't prepared me. There is no preparing. Nothing I can do. Nothing in this world could make it any less unbearable if I find out . . . if she's really . . . There's nothing else I can do."

"What if you never know for sure?" he said.

"Won't stop 'til I do."

We fell silent a moment—something I was grateful for.

The rural road was flat and straight and desolate, our solitary car the only vehicle, its half headlights made even fainter by the fog.

Thanks to Henry Folsom, we not only had a full tank of gas, but ration tickets to spare.

To conserve rubber for the war effort, I was supposed to be keeping it under thirty-five. I was doing nearly double that.

I thought of Lauren, of just how much I loved her, wanted her, needed her, of how I had to find her, of how I couldn't think of anything else.

Since the death of my dad when I was a kid, the only time I had felt safe, connected, and truly happy was when I had been with Lauren—and I had never, not in my entire life, felt as loved or in love, as possessing or possessed.

"Nothing matters but finding her," I said. "Nothing. What-ifs don't matter. Whether Harry was telling the truth doesn't matter. Nothing. Can't do anything to change whether I'm gonna find her dead or alive. All I can do is find her. Won't stop until I do and I'll do anything I have to."

"Anything, huh?"

"Those aren't just words," I said.

"I know you," he said. "I know they's shit you won't do."

"Not this time. Not when—"

"You'a beat up a bitch?"

I nodded.

He shook his head. "You wouldn't even slap hell outta one and you talkin' 'bout beatin' a bitch up."

"There's nothing I won't do."

"They's plenty you won't do," he said. "And that what worries me. What always worry me with you."

"Clip, I'm telling you—"

"You tellin' me what? That you'a cut a bitch? Sucker punch a stiff? Back-shoot a bastard? Kill a kid? Shee-it. They's plenty you won't do. Don't tell me they ain't."

I didn't respond.

Beyond the windows on both sides, silent trees streaked by like black lines on black paper, so impressionistic as to seem imaginative.

"Ain't sayin' it wrong. Hell, it part of why I even associate with your white ass. But don't say it ain't so. Knowing what you'a do and not do the difference between—"

"There a point to all this?"

"Not everybody cut out for every kind of work."

"You think I'm not up for this?"

"Think you needs to be clear on what you up for and what you ain't."

"I'm clear," I said.

"So shut the hell up, Clip," he said, smiling, his large bright white teeth seeming to light up the car. "Be seen and not heard like some docile house nigger."

"Something like that, yeah," I said with a small smile of my own.

"I can do that," he said.

"The hell you can."

He smiled again. Even bigger this time.

When Clip smiled with genuine amusement he looked like a mischievous young boy. Charming. Irrepressible. Full of himself.

We were both in bad shape, having run afoul of a Nazi nurse named Christa, a serial sex killer named Flaxon De Grasse, and various members of their twisted little surrealism society, and the moment of levity, the chance to smile, and the slight release of tension, was welcome and briefly buoying.

Maybe Clip was right. Maybe my moral code was a liability in looking for Lauren. Maybe I wasn't up for what would inevitably have to be done. I certainly wasn't physically.

I was useless enough without my right arm, but to also be injured, to be so completely depleted and thoroughly spent, to be banged up and bruised, to have an abdominal wound from getting gut shot actually seeping through the bandages at the moment, meant I couldn't look out for myself let alone save Lauren, but it didn't matter. I couldn't stop, could do nothing but what I was doing. No matter how many moral, emotional, and physical limitations I had to do it with.

"I've got to do this," I said.

"I know," he said, "and not just 'cause you done tol' me a few hundred times."

"Wasn't finished."

"Beg pardon. Please proceed."

"I've got to, but you don't. I know you think you owe me, but you don't. Never did."

"You think I tryin' to square the Dixon thing?"

A year or so back, when I was still part of PCPD, a couple of cops got the goods on Clip—something they'd been trying to do for a while. Wasn't much to it—some stolen merchandise Clip had little or nothing to do with—but that didn't matter. The two cops, Whitfield and Dixon, were just looking for a way in and they found it. Stolen merchandise was just their invite. Word was Clip had been sleeping with Dixon's wife. And I could tell by the way they were working the case they had no intention of taking it to trial. What they did intend was to tuck Clip in all nice and cozy to sleep the big sleep—probably making it look like he was killed trying to escape.

I had intervened and stopped them, and Clip had acted like he owed me ever since.

"The thought had occurred to me, yeah," I said.

"Well, I ain't. Least not the way you think."

"Oh yeah?"

"Yeah," he said, shaking his head. "I always be thinkin' you smarter than what you really is."

I laughed. "You're not the first to make that mistake."

We fell silent a moment.

In the dim spill of our half headlights, deer could be seen grazing the cold, damp grass on the soft shoulder of the road, their heads raising up, alerting on the light and noise as the car passed by.

I waited but he didn't say anything.

"Well?"

"Well what?"

"You gonna spill or what?"

"No," he said. "No sir, I is not. But I will tell you two things. One—I don't owe you shit. Two—I'm all in on this thing. Ask me about it again and I'a shoot your ass."

I nodded, not mentioning that was three things.

"Don't think my black ass don't know that was three things," he said.

"You not gonna answer me that, then tell me this."

He slid his hand inside his coat toward the Walther holstered there.

"Don't shoot," I said. "It's a different subject."

"What's that?"

"You never told me."

"What?"

"Were you giving little Clip to Dixon's little Mrs.?"

"Shee-it. Nothin' little about either. Betty Dixon thick as hell—way I like 'em—and if they was anything small about big Clip her husband wouldn't'a wanted to snuff out a nigger's pilot light, would he? 'Sides, you don't believe a brother, all you gots to do is aks your mom."

"Nice."

He smiled.

Mention of Mom reminded me just how long it'd been since I'd spoken to her, and I felt a sharp pang of guilt, but it was short lived, quickly replaced with loss and longing, anger and frustration.

"Much as I like talkin' about thick white women and my big black Clip, how's about you tell me the plan."

"Find her."

He nodded and smiled. "How we gonna do that?"

"Not sure exactly."

"The hell we headed to Tallahassee for?" he said.

I hadn't realized I hadn't told him, and it meant all the more that he was with me, that he was all in without even knowing what *in* was or where we were headed.

"It's the last place I know for sure she was," I said.

The night Lauren and I had left together, it was to get medical treatment at Johnston's Sanatorium in Tallahassee. After passing out and crashing my car into the main entrance, I had spent two days in a coma and a few more days after that in a drug-induced stupor. When I came out of it, I was told Lauren had been dead on arrival.

"If Harry took her from there and had her pronounced DOA, somebody had to help. Somebody knows something. We're gonna persuade them to tell us what. While we do that, Folsom's searching for De Grasse."

Flaxon De Grasse was a sadistic sex killer who drained all the blood from his bisected victims before displaying them in artistic poses and photographing them. Pale, white, bloodless bodies, black hair on heads and pubes, body parts arranged on a black satin backdrop—a demented surrealist artist creating with actual girls, all of whom, not coincidentally, resembled Lauren. He had yet to be apprehended, and not only did he pose a potential threat to Lauren, he might actually know where she was. He either had something to do with what had happened to her or was connected to those who did.

"There're a few other leads and probably several I haven't thought of," I said, "but these seem—"

I stopped speaking when the patrol lights lit up the inside of our car like a night carnival and the inside of my head with an all too familiar dread.

Chapter 2

"Where's the fire, fella?"

The middle-aged man had taken his time walking the short distance from his car to ours, his ambling, awkward movements disjointed in the strobe of the flashing lights.

He was square, flat, and tall, his sheriff's deputy uniform looking like it had been fitted over a thin, wide pine board.

We were idling on the side of Highway 20 next to a pasture, cows close enough to the fence to be seen in the revolving patrol lights and heard over the hum of the engines.

Before I could respond he said, "License and registration, and keep your hands where I can see 'em. Oh, your hand I mean, soldier. Didn't mean any disrespect."

As I slowly and awkwardly used my left to dig the wallet out of my coat pocket, he shone his flashlight beam around the car as best he could, searching the floorboards and backseat before letting it come to rest on Clip.

"Whatta we have here?" he said.

One look at Clip and he straightened up, dropping his hand down near the butt of his revolver and letting it hover there.

"Let me aks you somethin'," Clip said. "I'd'a been drivin', you'd thought I's his chauffeur, wouldn't you?"

"You sassin' me, boy?"

"No suh, not tonight. Tonight I is a seen and not heard house nigger."

The deputy looked confused, but covered it with anger.

"What gives? You boys don't look so good. Y'all got rods under them coats? You look like the sort that would."

Beneath the anger there was a butterfly flutter of nervousness. You could hear it in the subtle tremble at the edge of his voice.

"Sir, I'm Jimmy Riley," I said. "I used to be on the force. I'm a private detective working on an extremely important case. We're in a hurry—"

"No shit you're in a hurry. I mean, hell, soldier, you know you're supposed to keep it under thirty-five. A PI? What's so hellfire important? Where you headed?"

"Tallahassee. I don't have time to explain. You can radio Panama City PD and talk to Henry Folsom. He'll tell you. We're on the level. I swear it."

"What's his story, your chauffeur? I know he ain't never been no cop. How'd he lose the eye?"

"I training to be a private eye like him," Clip said. "Nobody tol' me you can have two."

"It's my fault," I said. "I should've told him."

"Huh? Oh. A couple of comedians," the cop said. "That's what y'all are. I get it. You've got time to be funny just not to answer my questions, that it?"

"Sorry," I said. "We're so tired we're loopy and we're . . . We meant no harm. Please radio Henry Folsom so we can go."

"So you can go?" he said, his voice rising and filling with humorless amusement. "So what if he says you're who you say you are? So what then? You think you can do what you want in our county 'cause a cop in Panama says you're okay, pal?"

"Then write me a ticket," I said. "Just get on with it."

"Don't know how they do it where you come from, but over here we don't take orders from peepers. No matter how much of a hurry they're in."

"I just meant—"

"I know what you meant, fella, and I don't like it. Not one bit."

"Like I said, we're in a hurry. It's a matter of life and death. We're in search of a missing woman."

"There's blood on your shirt," he said, tension beginning to constrict his voice even more.

"It's mine. My bandage is leaking. I—"

"Step out of the vehicle very slowly," he said. "Both of you. Keep your hands where I can see 'em."

"Listen," I said. "We don't—"

"You listen to me, soldier," he said, removing his revolver from its holster. "I ain't asking and I won't say it again."

We did what he said—me moving first, Clip reluctantly following. When we were out, he motioned us to the back of the car.

"All right, let's have the heaters," he said. "Nice and slow."

I knew Clip wouldn't surrender his under any circumstances. It had gotten me into more than a few jams over the past year or so. No matter the situation. No matter the stakes. Clip would never surrender his weapon. Not ever. And it was going to get us killed.

"Not me," Clip said. "I got mines off a dead man and'll be a dead man 'fore somebody get it off me."

"He means it," I said. "I wish right now he didn't, but I know for a certainty he does."

"Well, I mean to take it, soldier. I'm a man means what he says too. I'm gonna get your gun off you. Even if there's only one way to do it. Ain't no nigger gonna tell me he won't obey a lawful order. No sir."

"Look," I said, reaching into my pocket.

He brought his gun up and pointed it directly at me.

"Here's Henry Folsom's card. How about you call him instead of getting shot."

"I won't be the one to get shot," he said.

"Don't be so sure," Clip said, his Walther pointed at the cop's head.

"What the hell," he said. "How'd you—"

As he started to turn his gun toward Clip, I withdrew mine—though not as quietly or quickly as Clip had.

"Don't do it," Clip said to him, taking a step toward him and extending his gun another few inches.

The cop stopped in mid turn, his weapon pointed in between us. When he looked back at me, his eyes grew wide to see that I was holding a gun of my own.

"You gettin' better at gettin' that out with your left," Clip said.

"I stay up nights working on it," I said. "Soon all the ladies will call me Quickdraw Riley."

"They say you too quick with somethin', but it ain't you gun."

I returned my attention to the cop.

"We got the drop on you, partner," I said. "Good thing for you we're the good guys—"

"Shee-it," Clip said. "Speak for yourself."

"Good thing for you I'm one of the good guys and mean you no harm. Now, radio Panama City PD. Talk to Folsom and let's all live a little longer. Whatta you say?"

"I ain't puttin' my gun down," he said.

"You will if I tell you to," Clip said. "Ain't no coon ass country motherfucker gonna disobey an unlawful order I give."

"You don't have to," I said.

"Long as you don't point it at me," Clip said.

"Radio Folsom," I said.

He backed toward his car, keeping his gun pointed somewhere between us as he did. Standing behind his open door, he reached down into his car, retrieved the mic, and made the call.

The dark December night was cold, the wind a bit biting—causing my every aching cell to ache a little extra.

The flashing lights made me dizzy and the cop difficult to see, and I wondered if he was contemplating shooting at us from the cover of his car.

In the field the cows lowed—*mrurr, mrurr, mrurr*—and at least one of them had a bell that clanged dully as it moved about.

One shuddered and its muscles could be heard shaking, sounding like the low rumbling of thunder in the distance.

I stepped a few feet closer to the cop and I could hear him talking to Henry Folsom.

When he finished, he tossed the handset back onto the seat of the car, holstered his weapon, and stepped out from behind the door.

"Sorry fellas, but I had to be sure," he said. "You understand. Turns out Captain Folsom's a good friend of Sheriff Tatum. Good luck with finding the—"

Just then his head exploded and he collapsed to the pavement, as other rounds began to ring out and ricochet around us.

Chapter 3

With only a split second to determine where the shots were coming from, Clip and I both dove in the ditch behind our car, each of us with our backs against a wheel.

Rounds continued to ricochet around us.

Glass shattered and rained down on the ground. Divots of dirt flew up. Fence posts splintered. Sparks shot up from the pavement.

"How many you figure?" I asked.

"Least two. Too many shots, too fast, too close together to be one. Maybe three. Set up across the street."

The lowing of the cows and the clanging of the bell intensified. *Mrurr. Mrurr. Mrurr.*

"Keep shooting like this," I said, "they'll be out of ammo soon."

"Lessen they brought a armory wit 'em," Clip said. "Think this got anything to do with us, or just about square pants over there?"

"No way to know for sure, but think if it was just about him, they'd've waited 'til we were gone."

"Lessen they underestimate who he pulled over out here in the middle of nowhere."

We had yet to return fire, waiting for them to run out of rounds or make a move.

Just then a round hit one of the cows and it bellowed loudly as it hit the ground, continuing to moo and moan after it did.

"Motherfuck almighty," Clip said. "Bastards just dropped a cow."

"I saw that."

"May be time for us to start shooting back, they gonna shoot cows and shit."

"Can you see anything?" I asked.

We both turned slightly to get a better view, searching all around us for sight of the shooters.

"Can I see anything," Clip said. "Motherfucker I gots one eye and it ain't all that good."

From beneath the car, I could see the barrel of a rifle in the opposite ditch when the flashing light glinted off it, but that was it.

"Anything?" I said.

"Tol' you I can't see for shit."

He was looking around the back of the car, most of his body still behind the tire.

"Look like one of 'em 'bout to try to sneak up behind the patrol car."

"Got a shot?"

"Will."

"I've got a shooter in the ditch down a little ways. Let's take 'em at the same time. You say when."

I turned and lay facedown on the ground, the cold earth damp and bracing on my body, the pressure on my wound making me wobbly even lying down. Reaching beneath the car, I extended my arm and the revolver as far as I could, using the ground to steady my arm, and thumbed back the hammer.

In the far distance, I could see the first faint hint of headlights approaching from the east.

"Car coming," I said. "Need to go as soon as we can."

"On three," he said.

"Okay."

I waited, but he didn't say anything.

Rounds continue to pock surfaces around us.

Eventually, he said, "One."

I adjusted my grip on the gun. I had never been a great shot and I couldn't shoot for shit with my left, but my left was all I had.

"Two."

Just aim at the barrel. When the balloon goes up, squeeze off five fast rounds.

"Three."

In my periphery, I could see Clip jump up.

We both began firing at nearly the exact same moment.

They fired back at first, then no return fire, then we were out, then nothing.

"Got him," Clip said as he dropped back down behind the car. "You?"

"Can't tell. Be lucky as hell if I did. Was just firing at the glint of a barrel. Never saw anything else."

We waited.

No shots, no bell, just the lowing of the cows, the hum of the motors, and the mechanical whir and tick of the revolving lights.

"Hear that?" Clip asked. "Least they shot the one

wearing the bell."

We waited some more.

The lights of the approaching car grew closer and closer until it arrived. It slowed but didn't stop, then sped up, continuing away from us, west, in the direction we had come from.

In another moment, a car about a hundred feet down on the opposite side of the road cranked and raced away east toward Hosford, its lights only coming on after it was already a piece down the road.

Slowly, cautiously, we came out from behind the car to survey the scene.

We had each gotten our man. Clip's was on the ground behind the patrol car, mine, slumped in the ditch.

"Looks like you got yours," Clip said.

"More likely he shot himself," I said. "Or one of yours ricocheted off your guy and hit him."

"Guess there was a third shooter or a driver waiting in the car. We goin' after him?"

I shook my head. "Gonna radio Folsom. Give him the lay of the land here, then continue on where we were headed."

And after I spoke with Henry Folsom and he agreed to make everything jake with the Liberty County sheriff and clean up our mess, we did.

Chapter 4

Nancy Pippen wasn't the best nurse I had at Johnston's Sanatorium, but she was the most vulnerable, which made her the best place to start.

When her shift ended, she walked quickly and nervously toward her blue 1940 Pontiac Torpedo, scanning the street and actually looking over her shoulder a time or two as she did.

The nervousness was new. So was the over-the-shoulder paranoia. When I was a patient here what I had observed was an insecure, self-conscious young woman. What she was now went way beyond that.

She was extremely thin and pale, her long, narrow face jutting down into a pointy chin, her blond, pompadour-styled hair mostly hidden by her white nurse's cap.

While Henry Folsom worked on cleaning up the mess we'd made on Highway 20 in Liberty County, Clip and I had come to pay a call on Nervous Nancy.

Having just pulled up and parked less than a minute before she'd walked out, we'd nearly missed her—something Clip would've sworn was my fault because of how little help I had been in changing the two shot-out tires, a process that actually involved stealing one of the tires from the Liberty County deputy's car.

When she reached her vehicle and saw me, she jumped.

"Sorry," I said. "I didn't mean to startle you. Do you recognize me?"

She squinted a bit, her small blue eyes nearly disappearing. As her gaze drifted from my face to the folded coat sleeve where my right arm should have been, it came to her, her eyes widening, mouth opening.

Now she looked even more frightened than before.

"You're . . . you crashed your car into . . . You just disappeared . . . you're wanted by the police."

Her blue nurse's uniform was pressed, its white apron immaculate. It hung loosely on her slight frame, but couldn't hide the way her body shivered.

The night was dark, the temperature dropping, the blackout leaving little in the way of inadvertent illumination. The street was empty. The only sound was that of the wind—and very faintly in the distance a siren.

"You cold, or scared?" I asked.

"Both."

"I'm not here to hurt you," I said. "I'm no longer wanted by the police. I was kidnapped from your hospital. I've been through a thing or three lately. Sorry I look so bad, but I'm one of the good guys. I swear it."

She considered me a moment, then let her gaze drift around the area as if looking for help.

"If I were here to hurt you, I could have already," I said. "I just have a couple of questions for you. Can we sit in your car?"

She seemed so scared and frail I felt bad for her.

Hearing Clip walk up behind her, she turned, and as she saw him, she fainted. I caught her as best I could with one arm, then Clip helped me get her in the car.

Groggy confusion quickly gave way to startled recognition then fear.

We had her in the backseat. We were in the front. Clip in the driver's seat, I in the passenger's, both of us turned back toward her.

She started to try to push my seat up in order to get out, but realized how futile it was, then sat back and began to cry softly.

"Nancy," I said. "I'm not here to hurt you. I swear. I just have some questions for you. You passed out. We could've taken you. We didn't. We're in your car. You're safe. Just answer my questions and we'll be gone."

She didn't respond, just continued to cry quietly.

I waited.

Eventually, she said, "Why is all this happening?"

"All what?"

"All of it."

"I'm gonna need you to be a little more specific," I said.

"Did y'all kill her?"

"Who?" I asked. "We haven't killed anyone."

Clip looked over at me, both his brows and the corners of his mouth twitching ever so slightly toward a smile.

"So many bad things are happening," she said.

"I don't understand. We didn't do anything. She didn't deserve—"

"Who was killed?" I asked.

"Betty Jane. Murdered."

"She the short brunette nurse with the Boston accent?"

"Busybody Betty we called her," she said. "Always gettin' into something. You know the type."

"She was killed?"

She nodded. "Here in the sanatorium. Stabbed to death. It was the most horrible thing I've ever seen."

"You saw it happen?"

"What? No. I caught a glimpse of her when they were trying to revive her. There was so much blood."

"Who did it?"

"We don't know, but everything happened after you . . . after the night of your wreck. That's when it all started. I heard some of the other girls talking. They said it had something to do with you."

"What else has happened?"

"Just strange stuff. It's in the air. Something's going on. Everybody's on edge. Whispering. Speculating. Acting so different. One of the other nurses went missing."

"Who?"

"Doris," she said. "Doris Perkins. Didn't show up for her shift one day. Hasn't been seen or heard from since last week."

"You were working the night I arrived, right?"

She nodded.

"There was a woman with me," I said.

"Yes, Lauren," she said. "I'm awful sorry for what happened. It was so sad. It was obvious how much you loved her. I can't tell you how many times you said her name—called for her, reached for her—half-conscious, unconscious, awake, asleep. Didn't matter. I don't know what y'all were mixed up in, but I know real love when I see it. Hope somebody loves me like that one day."

"What exactly happened to her?" I asked.

"Well . . . whatta you mean? She died, mister."

"Was she dead when we arrived?"

"She was in real bad shape, but she wasn't dead. I heard her moan and say something about a soldier."

Something inside me broke open and I felt like I took my first real breath since waking from the coma. I knew I shouldn't let myself hope, knew how counterproductive, even dangerous, to my mission it could be, but I couldn't help it.

"She was alive when we arrived?"

"For a little while, yes."

"What happened?" I said. "Tell me everything."

"All I know is what we did to you. I was assigned to your surgery. When we took you to the operating room, they hadn't really moved her yet."

"Why do you think she died?"

"They told us she did," she said. "When we came out of surgery. I have no idea if they even got her out of the car before it happened. Don't know exactly what happened to her."

"Who would?" I said. "Who was working on her?"

Her eyes grew wide and her mouth dropped open in realization.

"Let me guess," Clip said. "Busybody Betty and Disappearing Doris."

She nodded. Slowly. Deliberately. Devastatingly.

Chapter 5

"**W**ait," Nancy said. "We had a negro on the ward that night."

"Congratulations," Clip said.

"No. I mean there was a negro nurse because of it. Army nurse. Brought in to take care of a negro serviceman. It was . . . Everything happened so fast. And we were short staffed. She shouldn't have, but it was crazy—she . . . I saw her helping out with Lauren."

It was no surprise that it stood out to her. There were very few negro nurses in the army, but a negro serviceman would require a negro nurse.

"She wasn't here long, because he wasn't," she said. "He should've never been here at all, but it couldn't be helped."

Black nurses were rare, but so were black servicemen. Though many tried to enlist, few were allowed to, especially by the local draft boards run by whites in the South. The general perception by white people in our area was that blacks were disloyal, lazy, cowards, intellectually inferior, unfit to serve.

For the few actually accepted, they were mostly

assigned non-essential roles and menial duties, becoming waiters and cooks, janitors and maintenance workers, and musicians in service bands. Segregation laws and the Jim Crow system in the South meant that white and black servicemen had not "closed ranks" as W.E.B. DuBois had encouraged during World War I.

"What's her name?" I asked.

"Bernice Baker."

"Where can I find her?"

Her eyes narrowed and her pointy chin jutted forward a bit and she looked at me like I had just asked her to consider joining the Nazi party.

"I have absolutely no idea," she said. "Why would I?"

"Think," I said. "I've got to find her. Did she ever say anything? Did you ever overhear anything?"

"No, but our cook is a negro. He might know."

"'Cause we all know each other," Clip said.

Augustus Jackson was a large, slow-moving man with a huge head and hands the size of catchers' mitts. His too tight white uniform was soiled, its seams fighting a losing battle that would be over soon and wouldn't end well for the garment.

We found him in the kitchen, humming to himself as he cleaned up from the evening meal.

"Sorry suh," he said when he saw me, "but kitchen closed. Be serving breakfast bright and—"

He stopped talking when Clip walked in behind me.

"Clipper Jones," he said with genuine delight. "How

the hell you been, boy?"

I looked over at Clip. "Y'all know each other?" I asked with a smile.

"All right, boss," he said to Jackson, ignoring me. "How about you?"

"You know, just old. Gettin' older every second. Near about out of my prime now."

"Not even close according to all these little white nurses runnin' 'round here."

Jackson frowned and cut his eyes over, indicating me.

"He all right. Whatcha been up to? 'Sides being thigh high in white pussy."

"It's all pink, boy," Jackson said. "You ever get any, you'll see."

I laughed out loud at that.

"Look like you'd get a little sympathy slim just from the eye," he added.

"Would, wouldn't it?" Clip said.

Jackson shook his head and smiled. "Nah, still just slingin' slop for the sick and dyin'."

"Maybe it your slop what killin' 'em," Clip said. "Thought of that?"

He smiled. "It's been suggested before, boy. Don't think you's the first."

"This here Jimmy Riley," Clip said, nodding toward me. "He a detective lookin' for a nigger."

"Heard of you," he said. "And not just from Clipper here, but talk around this place. You's here not too long ago."

I nodded.

"Army nurse here the night I arrived," I said.

"Baker."

"What you need her for?"

"Questions about that night," I said. "That's all."

He looked at Clip. Clip nodded.

"That's easy," he said. "She be over to the jook tonight."

Chapter 6

Juke joints or "jooks" began in the South in sharecropper shacks as places where blacks could congregate, drink, dance, and socialize out of the sight of whites.

Birthplace of the blues, a jook was little more than a ramshackle room with a few Christmas lights strung up, a place for a local or traveling band to play, space for dancing, maybe a few mismatched chairs and tables, and a small crowd of people checking the injustices of their lives at the door.

These days jukes were a little more sophisticated, but not much.

Bud's Beer and Barbeque looked to be a converted service station, its intact overhang serving both as a covered porch and a place to tack up advertisements for everything from beer and cigarettes to war bonds and upcoming bands.

Even from the damp dirt and mud hole parking lot, you could tell Bud's was hopping tonight. Ginned-up hep cats and kittens, young and old, soldiers and civilians, spilled out of the joint with the sounds of blues-infused jazz and the laughs and shouts, whoops and hollers of people having a good time.

The raucous crowd, both inside and out, lived up to what I had read about joints like this and reminded me that the term *juke* was said to have come from a Gullah word that means rowdy or disorderly.

Gullah, the Creole language spoken by Southern negroes living by the sea, could still be heard on occasion, its influence lingering on. It was most commonly used by slaves in the Carolinas, Georgia, and North Florida in the eighteenth and nineteenth centuries.

When I parked, Clip said, "I'a get this one. Be right back with her."

"Why?"

He looked at me like it was obvious. "Figured you might be more comfortable waiting here."

I shook my head.

"Well, hell, let's go," he said. "Not like anything bad ever happen to a white man in a place like this."

I smiled.

"Nah," he said. "It'a be fine. Ain't nobody gonna pay you no mind."

As we approached the place, I got a few sideways glances, but no overt glares or hostility. More than a few men nodded their heads and most of the women smiled.

The missing arm and my overall compromised and disheveled appearance had to help. I may have represented oppression, but it was obvious I posed no threat to anyone—except maybe myself.

Inside, the relatively small room was packed with people. Dancing. Drinking. Talking and carrying on. The five-piece band was set up in the back left corner. Diagonally across from them in the opposite corner, a group of men sat around a table playing poker. And though there were a few other chairs and tables spread randomly throughout the room with people on and around them, it seemed as if everyone else was moving.

The moment we stepped through the door, a thick young woman with a smallish waist and large, pointy breasts buzzed a beeline for us from the back of the room.

A few more looks here and there, but mostly everybody paid me no mind.

As far as I could tell I wasn't just the palest face in the room, I was the only white one.

"Clipper Jones," she said. "Where ya been keepin' yourself, *baby*?"

"Been around," he said. "Busy working my way back to you, girl."

"Took you long enough, *shuga*."

She emphasized *shuga* the same way she had *baby*, her voice rising an octave and stretching it out, her mouth making it sexy and seductive.

"Came back as fast as I could."

"Who dis?" she asked. "He cute."

She wore a light blue dress just a bit too small and black heels too narrow for her feet and too tall for her frame.

"This here Jimmy," he said. "Jimmy, this here Nadine."

"How'd you lose your arm, soldier?"

Before I could respond, a tall, narrow nervous-looking negro came up with a small suitcase of liquor and cigarettes.

"Drink, soldier?"

I looked at Clip, eyebrows up, asking not if but what.

"Let us get a bottle of that bourbon," he said.

I looked at Nadine.

"I's partial to that Dixie Belle gin, baby."

I pulled out some of Harry's money, bought the bottles and gave him a big tip.

"Thank ya, suh," he said, and moved off.

"I'm looking for someone," I said to Nadine.

"You found her," she said.

I smiled. "It's very important."

Clip said, "You seen a nurse named Bernice Baker?"

She shook her head, her eyes still fixed on me. "No sir, I don't believe I ever have."

"You sure?" I asked.

She seemed to think about it a little more. "Sorry. Don't know her."

"Okay. Thanks."

We began moving away from her.

"Wait," she said.

We turned back toward her.

"That all y'all wanted me fo? Sniffin' after some nursin' nigger?"

"That's it," Clip said. "Least you got a bottle of gin out of it."

She huffed away and we pressed further in.

We moved around the dancing, drinking, rollicking, frolicking crowd asking after Bernice Baker and coming up with nothing.

"Place this small," Clip said, "crowd this close, either she ain't ever been here or we being lied to."

"Which you think?" I asked.

Before he could answer, an extremely large, muscular man in nothing but overalls and brogans pushed a few people aside and stood in front of me, flexing confrontationally.

There was something about him—the shape of his head, face, and features, and the way one of his eyes wandered—that hinted at a lack of intelligence or worse, but more troubling was the very real meanness and menace present too.

Those dancing closest to us stopped and began gathering around, believing something worth seeing was about to happen.

"Dis ain't da place for you," he said. "You needs to git on out from up in here."

The big man's body looked as thick and hard as a live oak tree, large, snaking veins showing beneath his dark, glistening skin. His arms looked like anacondas ready to attack, and real madness glinted in his too close eyes.

Clip shook his head. "They's always one. Always. Always gots to be one nigger in every crowd gonna act the fool."

At that, more people stopped dancing and gathered around.

"You only git one chance to leave on your own, mister," he said. "I hate to mess up the good time dese nice folk be havin', but you don't git on from up in here now, you ain't gonna be able to on your own."

Now no one was dancing and the crowd around us pressed in even closer, pushed, no doubt, by those behind them.

"So I's clear," Clip said, "that go for both of us or just him?"

Without looking away from me, the man hit Clip so fast and so hard I'd swear he'd had professional boxing training. The blow landed right on the sweet spot, rocking Clip's chin, jerking his head to the side and causing his knees to buckle. He collapsed to the floor, unmoving, unconscious.

The music stopped. The room went still and silent.

I glanced down at Clip again, willing him to get up. Nothing. He had yet to move or make a sound.

Chapter 7

"Dere go his answer," he said. "What gonna be yours?"

"Hey, come on, Deek," a short, squat young man in alligator shoes said as he stepped in between us. "There's no need for that."

"Don't put yor hands on me, Charlie," Deek said.

Charlie had his hands up, but wasn't touching Deek and seemed to know better.

"Deek, you know I know better than to touch you. Now come on, big fella, leave these men in peace."

"Dey de ones leavin'," he said. "And fast."

Charlie turned to me. "Bernice my aunty. What you lookin' for her for?"

"Just to ask her a few questions about a patient she saw at Johnston's Sanatorium while she was there," I said. "That's it. Not looking to put her in a jam. She hasn't done anything wrong. She may not even know much, but if she does, that's all I need—a little information."

"Okay, I'll take you to her, mister," he said. "Keep anybody else from getting hurt or killed. All right?"

"Thanks," I said.

"I'll even help you get your friend to the car and

make sure he okay, okay?"

"Okay."

He turned back to Deek. "Okay with you, big fella?"

"Just git 'em the fuck outta here," he said. "And fast."

Most everyone was still gawking at Clip, who had yet to move. The music was still silent and an awkward muteness had made its way in and hung palpably above and around the people.

"All right, everybody," Charlie yelled. "Go on back to dancin'. This all over. Nothin' to see." He looked over at the band. "Well, play, damn it."

They did, and as soon as the music had a full head of steam, people slowly began to drift away, a few even beginning to dance again—though without much conviction.

As promised, Charlie helped me gather Clip, but when he saw how I was struggling with my half, he yelled for another man to take my place.

Clip regained consciousness as he was dragged across the dance floor, the tops of his shoes scraping the bare wood, but he was clearly still dazed and had yet to regain his wits or equilibrium.

By the time we were outside, he was no longer dragging his feet, and when we reached the car, he was standing on his own.

The man who had helped Charlie had broken off the moment Clip was walking on his own and was almost back inside now. Charlie was standing with us next to our car in the dark parking lot.

I knew what no one else here knew. I knew that Clip had spent most of the previous day bound and gagged in the trunk of a car and had nearly died. I knew that he was weak and a good step slower than normal. I knew that was why Deek was able to catch him the way he did. And I knew Clip would never mention it, that it would never even cross his mind that he had a legitimate excuse for what had happened.

"You okay?" I asked.

"Won't be 'til that nigger in the ground," he said.

I also knew he could never let something like that go unresponded to.

All the men I knew worth anything at all as men had certain nonnegotiables—lines we drew in the sands of our lives. Things we would do and not do. Things we would allow to be done to us and things we would not. Mine and Clip's were different but we both had them. That's why he had asked me earlier what I was willing to do to find Lauren, why he hadn't believed me when I said I would do anything.

What we lived for, what we were willing to die for, made us the men we were. Where we drew the lines of our lives was what defined us, was what distinguished us from other sorts of men. Something Emerson had said on the subject had always stuck with me. Nothing is at last sacred but the integrity of a man's own mind. Something like that.

Clip's lines included never surrendering his weapon and never letting a man put his hands on him. He had other lines, of course, but these two were big bold lines, the basis for many of the others.

Charlie shook his head, his eyes wide. "Let it go, brother. He ain't a nigger to be fucked with."

"No," Clip said, "you got that backward. I ain't a nigger to be fucked with."

"He'll kill you," Charlie said.

"No, what he'a do is sucka punch a nigga. I'a kill one."

I knew those weren't just words for Clip, not an idle threat, but what he intended to do. I also knew there was nothing I could do to change his mind or stop him—short of killing him.

Headlights of leaving and arriving cars illuminated small parts of the lot, the weak beams gliding across parked cars—some of them with lovers leaning on them—and small groups of people smoking and sharing a bottle. It was colder now, a brisk breeze winding its way around and in between the vehicles and people.

Out here the music was muted but could still be heard. Somewhere in the dark lot a bottle broke and a girl laughed loudly. In the distance a dog barked.

"Even if you could kill him, and you can't," Charlie said, "you can't kill a man for punching you."

"You let any man put his hands on you, you gots to be willin' to let every man," Clip said. "I ain't that kind of nigger."

"But—"

"Ain't got time to teach you how to be a man right now," Clip said.

"I can't just let you kill a man," Charlie said.

"You welcome to go warn him."

Charlie looked at me. "Talk to him. He's still punch-drunk from the shot he took."

I locked eyes with Charlie and said, "'Comes a time in every man's education when he arrives at the conviction that envy is ignorance, that imitation is suicide, that he must take himself for better for worse as his portion.'"

He looked confused.

"More Emerson."

"Huh?"

"Did the fact that I said *more* confuse you?" I asked. "It was just that I had quoted some earlier in my head."

"Say what?"

"He read a lot," Clip said. "Jimmy know he got no chance of talking me out of this."

I did. I knew it to a certainty—a certainty like I knew few things in life.

I nodded.

Clip had a way of living. He knew of nor was interested in no other. He had no back-down in him, no compromise, no matter the cost. He'd die first. I had no doubt that eventually his death before (what he considered) dishonor conviction would get him killed—and maybe me too—and I also knew he was as resigned to that as anything in his life.

I couldn't say I understood exactly why Clip was the way he was. I knew it involved pride, but it wasn't just that, wasn't as simple as that. I knew he couldn't live with himself if he couldn't live this way. I couldn't say we were identical on this particular point. But I could say it made a certain sense to me. Like Clip, there were things I was willing to die for. They were just somewhat different things—though not that different—and not as many.

"Would you just help me find Lauren first?" I said.

"This can't wait," he said.

"It's gonna make what we're doing more difficult and it's difficult enough. Maybe even impossible."

"Can't be helped," he said. "I didn't deal the play, but I damn sure gonna play the hand."

I nodded.

"You go on and talk to Miss Bernice," he said. "I'a catch up with you later."

I shook my head.

"Can't take a chance on—"

"I can't leave," I said. "You know that."

He nodded.

"It's a good thing, 'cause I don't know no Miss Bernice," Charlie said. "I's just tryin' to get y'all up out of there."

I looked at him.

He nodded. "Got no Auntie Bernice. Sorry. Was just trying to save your life."

"Well, thanks for that," I said.

He shrugged it off and shot me a look of mild futility.

"Shit just got simple," Clip said.

"Oh yeah?" I asked in surprised amusement. "How's that?"

"We ain't got what we came for," he said. "So we go back in and get it. And if that big Farmer Brown motherfucker got anything to say about it, I'a deal with him."

"I'm sure he said all he had to say before," I said. "Sure he'll just let us go about our business."

"Well, let's just say he don't," Clip said. "You know, for the sake of argument. He start something again, maybe even take the first swing or stab or shot, it'a make you feel better 'bout me pine-boxing his ass. The result the same. I get what I want. You sleep better about it. Everybody happy."

"'Cept Farmer Brown," I said.

"Man, fuck him," he said. "I tired of tryin' to make everybody happy."

I smiled. "I know that's been a real big burden on you."

Chapter 8

When we walked back in the joint, Clip withdrew his
Walther and fired a round into the ceiling.

In an instant the place went still and silent, the band
stopping, the dancers halting, everyone looking at us.

Interestingly, no one screamed or ran. Just stood
there giving us their full attention.

It was just me and Clip, Charlie deciding not to come
back in with us. We were standing just inside the open
double doors of the entrance.

"Guess I wasn't clear before," Clip said. "Sorry 'bout
that. Sometimes I is just too damn subtle. We looking for
a missin' white woman. We think a nurse named Bernice
Baker might have some information we need to find her.
That's all. Miss Bernice, you here?"

No one said anything. No one stepped forward.

"Anybody here know Bernice Baker?"

Again no one said anything.

"I know you a dead nigger," Deek said.

Even back a little ways in the crowd with a couple
of rows of people in front of him, he was still visible, his
enormity unable to be completely hidden.

"Well, look here," Clip said. "If it ain't sucker puncher motherfucker. Why you so far back, boy? Quit hiding behind them women and step up so I can hear what you gots to say."

He didn't move.

"I here to do two things," Clip said. "Extinguish that big nigger's flame and find Miss Bernice Baker. Preferably in that order. Y'all move out the way so I can see his ugly ass since he too big a coward to come out hisself."

The people in front of him began moving away.

We stepped further inside, nearly to the center of the room.

"Who here know Miss Bernice?" Clip said.

No one indicated that they did.

"Y'all go on and git from in front of him," Clip said. "Don't want nobody gittin' hurt on accident."

They began moving a little quicker.

"Oh, you a big nigger now you got a gat in your hand?" Deek said.

He was standing alone now, no one within five feet of him in any direction.

"What you say, coward?" Clip said. "Step up here and die like a man."

"I'a step up there," Deek said. "Drop the rod."

Clip immediately dropped the gun on the floor, the heavy thud sounding like a shot ricocheting around the room.

He'd die before letting anyone take his weapon, but he'd drop it instantly if it suited his purpose—which at the moment was beating or killing the big negro in a fair fight.

At that I had expected Deek to rush him, but he didn't move.

"Thought the rod was keeping you away?" Clip said.

"Man, I ain't got time for this," he said.

"Oh, I'm keeping you from something?" Clip said. Then turning to me added, "He got somewhere to be."

Deek began slowly moving toward the door, giving Clip a wide berth as he did.

"You gonna have to shoot me in the back," he said. "I ain't standing around playin' the fool for you."

I hoped revealing Deek for the bullying coward he was would be enough for Clip, but I knew better.

"Probably best for you to die outside like a dog anyway," Clip said. "Not mess up this dance floor and these people's good time tonight."

When Deek was nearly parallel with us, he lunged at Clip, coming up with a small handgun as he did.

Firing as he ran, Deek missed Clip and me, but managed to wing a guy leaning on the wall behind us.

As he got closer and his empty pistol began dry firing, he lowered his shoulders and ducked his head down, crouching to tackle Clip, but just as he reached him, Clip shimmied and twisted, avoiding Deek altogether, then sticking his foot out and tripping him as he stumbled by.

Deek went down fast and hard, his thick, muscular body smacking the wood plank floor with such force it cracked a board.

"Once a motherfucker sucker puncher," Clip said, "always a motherfucker sucker puncher."

Stooping down, Clip picked up his pistol then walked over to Deek, holding the gun down beside him as he did.

Still facedown, Deek was just beginning to roll over. When he did finally manage to get on his back, he began pushing away from Clip in a kind of awkward crab crawl.

When he reached him, without saying a word, Clip raised the gun and pointed it at Deek's huge head.

As Clip began to squeeze the trigger, a middle-aged woman stepped over and said, "Wait. Don't shoot. I'm Bernice Baker. Don't shoot him."

"What about to happen to him got nothin' to do with you," Clip said. "Talk to Jimmy. He got a few questions for you."

"No, don't shoot," she said. "This my son Deek. He's just trying to protect his mama. Please don't kill him. Please. He's just lookin' out for his mama. Don't make him die for doing that."

I wasn't sure if that was enough to keep Clip from killing him. Before this moment, I would've said Deek was a dead man, but now there was a slight chance he might actually make it through the night.

Clip continued looking down at the man, who was panting heavily and avoiding eye contact.

Everyone waited.

Eventually, Clip took his finger off the trigger, lowered the gun, and extended his other hand to help Deek up.

Deek hesitated, but then took it.

Clip pulled him upright and the moment he was standing, flipped the Walther around in his hand and hit him in the center of his forehead with the butt of the weapon. He went down hard, unconscious by the time his head hit the floor again.

Chapter 9

"You didn't have to do that to my boy," Bernice Baker was saying.

We were back in the dark parking lot. Four guys had carried Deek out and he was lying on the front seat of his mom's car. Both doors were open to accommodate his length, his boots nearly touching the ground on the driver's side.

Bernice was squatted down in the V formed by the open passenger door, rubbing her son's head. Clip and I were standing a few feet away.

"You better just be glad he alive," Clip said.

"I am," she said. "Thank you for that."

"Why didn't you just talk to us?" I asked.

"I's scared to," she said.

"But you'll talk to us now?"

She nodded. "Everybody here already think I am. Might as well. You promise to leave my boy alone?"

"Yes ma'am," I said.

She looked up and over at Clip. "Wants to hear it from him."

He hesitated a moment then nodded. "Long as he

leave me alone."

"He will," she said. "Here, help me up."

She held her large, flappy arms up and we each took one.

Bernice Baker was an enormous woman with an ample ass, big breasts, and chubby black cheeks. Even her knees, which were visible just beneath her white cotton dress, were fat. They, along with other joints in her body creaked and popped as we helped her stand up. Her hair came down to near the bottom of her neck, and it, like her coal-black skin, looked oily, its moistness glinting in the little light there was.

"What are you afraid of?" I asked.

"Who you here looking for information about?"

"Lauren Lewis."

"Then you know."

She had just the hint of a lisp and her enormous lips, which were painted an extremely bright red, protruded in a kind of puckered pout, which conspired to make her challenging to understand.

"Wait," she said. "You were with her."

I nodded.

"You's in a bad way, fella," she said. "Don't look too much better now. Surprised to see you up and about."

"Tell me about Lauren," I said.

"Everything happen so fast," she said. "I was back in the colored section with this boy from Tuskegee when I heard a loud crash and yelling. I ran out to see what was going on. I shouldn't have. The rest of the hospital is whites only, but . . . I get out there and I see the car and the rubble and . . . at first I just stood there, but they's shorthanded so while the only doc and a nurse took you, I helped get the woman—Lauren—out of the car and onto a gurney. I heard someone say 'Do you know who that is?' but I didn't hear the reply. She was so beautiful."

"She was alive?" I asked. "You're sure?"

She nodded. "She's in bad shape. Same as you. But she was fightin' awfully hard. Wasn't studdin' no dying. Kept mumbling somethin' 'bout some serviceman."

Clip said, "Serviceman?"

"Somethin' like that."

"Soldier maybe?" he said.

"That it," she said. "Soldier."

Deek moaned a little but didn't stir.

"What happened next?" I asked.

"This all took a while," she said. "And they didn't really have nowhere to take her so we worked on her right there on the gurney. I's mostly watching—there if they needed me, but tryin' to stay out the way. Then one of the nurses said something to the other about callin' to let him know, and she left for a while. I helped a little during that time. Directly, she came back. 'Ventually a army nurse showed up and took over. Came in like she owned the place. Told me to return to the colored section. I did, but I was slow to do it, seeing what they's gonna do next. They rolled her down the other hall, but I didn't see where they took her from there. I knew there's somethin' wrong then, but I didn't know just how wrong 'til later."

"What'd you know then and what'd you find out later?" I asked. "Tell me everything. Every detail."

"Well, some Army nurse gonna come in and take over? And just how funny the other two nurses were acting—making a call in the middle of working on the poor girl? Who she gonna call? Makes no sense. Next day I hear that she didn't make it—which, with how she looked, I coulda believed, but they say she DOA. I know that wasn't right. So when I can, I pull the death certificate. They say she arrive dead, that she never regain consciousness. They got time of death a good hour before the last time I saw her alive. Then . . . you hear what happened to the two nurses what worked on her?"

I nodded.

"One murdered right there in the sanatorium, the other vanished without a trace. Somethin' ain't right with the whole deal. So don't blame me if I don't step forward when two thugs come looking for me."

"Thugs?" Clip asked with a smile.

"Thugs, gangsters, whatever."

"Actually," he said, "we the good guys."

Deek moaned some more, beginning to rouse. She looked down at him.

"Bet my baby have somethin' to say about that."

"Did you catch the army nurse's name?" I asked. "What'd she look like?"

"She introduced herself as Nurse Powell," she said.

That name was as haunted for me as any name I knew, its two syllables bearing with their breathed vibrations open wounds that ran like deep trenches down to some dark part of my unseen core.

"She listed on the death certificate as Valerie Powell," Bernice was saying. "She a stout white woman. Pale as hell. Light red hair. Heavy makeup she tryin' to cover freckles with but it didn't work."

She may have said more. Probably did. But if she did I didn't hear it.

Chapter 10

We found a payphone a few blocks down from the juke. I was using it to call Henry Folsom. Clip was in the car.

The darkness seemed somehow darker now.

The phone box was on a street corner near a closed service station, situated beneath a streetlamp, which was off.

Clip had the car idling, its half headlights placing the booth in a narrow arc of pale light, the distorted shadow it cast elongating and disappearing into the night. Beyond the booth, past the pallid patch of phosphorescence, there was nothing—no wide world, no living souls, no nocturnal activities. Nothing but night.

"Hiya Jimmy," Folsom said. "How's it going over there?"

I told him.

"So now we actually know for sure she was alive when y'all arrived that night. That's great news, son. Great news."

There was no cop I respected more than Henry Folsom. He was the most honest, hardworking, and humble I knew. He wasn't particularly well liked—turning in fellow cops for taking bribes, telling the mayor to go fuck himself, and following evidence even when it leads to the elite of the establishment won't win many friends—but he was respected by the honest and feared by the corrupt. He had always treated me more like a son than a subordinate—something that hadn't changed since I became a civilian again—and though he felt bad about me losing my arm while working for him, nothing he ever did for me felt like pity.

"I'm very happy for you, Jimmy," he was saying. "Very happy."

"Thank you," I said. "I'm trying not to think about it. Just focusing on finding her."

What Clip had said earlier was true. She could still be dead. Just because a negro nurse saw her or thinks she saw her alive at a certain point early after our arrival didn't mean Lauren was still alive.

"All you can do," he said. "Don't do anything but. And don't let your mind wander to what-ifs."

"Trying not to."

"You call me, you need to, fella," he said. "I'll straighten you right out. And fast."

"Thanks."

"You think the murder and the disappearance are connected to Lauren?"

"Hard not to," I said.

"Part of some kind of cover-up?" he said.

"That's what I'm thinking," I said. "Tell me if I'm trying to connect things that don't."

"No, I agree. I'll poke around a bit into the murder and see what I can dig up on the missing girl. What was her name again?"

"Doris Perkins."

"And I'll find an address on the Powell woman right away. You think she's even a real nurse?"

Like the first time I had heard her name, hearing reference to Valerie Powell reminded me of three dead people—Dorothy Powell, my old partner Ray Parker, our secretary July—and the events that seemed now to have happened a lifetime ago.

"Bernice didn't seem to doubt it."

"I've got a friend on the force over there. We should probably get him involved. I'll give him a call. He can help track this down for us and fill us in on where they are with the investigations."

"As long as it doesn't involve Collins," I said.

"Doesn't. Name is Dana Shelby. Detective. Good cop."

"Thanks," I said. "Speaking of friends, the thing in Liberty County squared away?"

"Spoke with the sheriff. We're gettin' it all straightened out. And working on identities for the two shooters."

We were quiet a moment. I wanted to thank him again, but felt like that was all I was saying to him these days and it was taking away from what I was actually trying to convey somehow.

"How's Clip holding up?" he asked. "Didn't look so good this morning."

It had been Folsom who had backed my play against Whitfield and Dixon when I intervened to keep Clip from getting framed and executed, and he had kept up with him ever since.

"He's okay," I said. "I think. Hard to tell with him."

"Let me know what y'all need, and keep checking in. I'll be here through the night. Not leaving."

"What about Gladys?"

It was the first time I had ever referred to his infirmed wife by her first name. I was taking a liberty, a leap of intimacy that felt warranted.

He had always been the one to care for her at night, never allowing anyone else to even lend the least bit of assistance, so I couldn't help but wonder who he was letting help him tonight.

He was quiet a long moment, and I thought I had crossed a line until I heard the way he cleared his throat.

"I finally had to put her in a place," he said, his voice discernibly weaker. "Got no one to go home to."

I had been so wrapped up in my own little affairs I hadn't even asked after her lately. If I had, I would've known.

"Oh, Chief," I said. "I'm so sorry."

"She's better off," he said. "They're doing far more for her than I could. I just . . ."

I waited a long moment, but he didn't say anything else.

Eventually, he said, "We're chasing down a few leads on De Grasse but they're long shots. Be surprised if anything comes of them."

"We've got to find her before he does," I said.

"You think he'll go after her?"

"The girls he killed were patterned after Lauren," I said.

"But wasn't that because Harry chose them?"

"It was," I said. "At least in part. But she's the ultimate end of what they were doing, the raison d'être,

64

meant to—"

"The what?"

"The reason for the entire thing," I said. "I think she was also meant to be the pièce de résistance."

"What's with all the French, fella?"

"Sorry," I said. "They're just the best phrases to express what I mean."

"All that readin' you do's got you so I don't understand you much of the time."

"I'm just saying she was the beginning and the end," I said. "As least as far as Harry was concerned. Does that change anything now that he's dead? I'm afraid that for someone like Flaxon De Grasse it doesn't. I see him as this obsessive collector who won't stop until he has the entire set of something. If that's true, Harry's death doesn't change anything. Lauren is still the denouement."

"There you go again."

I started to apologize, but heard the laugh in his voice and was glad for it.

From a few blocks down the street, headlights appeared. They were the first I'd seen since I'd been in the booth.

"We're gonna find him," he said. "Got roadblocks everywhere. He's not getting out of our town. We're gonna find him and we're gonna find her."

"Yes we are," I said.

The way I sounded bothered me but good. My words were weak and hollow, like empty bravado.

When the headlights arrived they were attached to an unmarked police car.

There were two cops in the car, neither friendly, both looking like they were looking for a fight. Both looking like they were pretty sure they had found one. They had pulled up beside Clip and shown a light at him, eyeing him suspiciously as they did.

"Can you call your friend in the force over here now?" I asked.

"Sure," he said "Why?"

"'Cause," I said, "I'm pretty sure we're gonna need him."

Chapter 11

By the time I was off the phone and stepping out of the booth, one of the two middle-aged cops was standing there.

"What gives, pal?" he said.

His dark suit covered a solid build—especially for a man his age—but in every other way he couldn't have been more average. Average height. Average weight. Average looks. And I suspected average intelligence.

The other cop, a tall, thin man with a hairline that started about halfway back on his head, had Clip out of the car, the mounted spotlight on his windshield still shining in Clip's face.

"One-eyed midnight over there," the cop closest to me said, jerking his head in Clip's direction. "He with you or threatening you?"

I looked over at Clip.

"Threatening me?" I asked.

"Looked to us like he was about to run you over with the car."

"Mr. Jones is with me," I said.

"Mr. Jones? Hear that Roy? That's Mr. Jones you got

there."

"How do you do, Mr. Jones?" Roy asked.

Clip didn't respond.

"Hey Sam, I'm not so sure Mr. Jones can speak. Maybe that eye ain't all he's missin'."

"'Less the nigger got no tongue he better speak when spoken to," Sam said to me in a low, mean voice.

I didn't say anything.

"Ask 'im again, Roy," Sam said.

"How do you do, Mr. Jones?"

"How do I do what?" Clip said.

"Sam, you hear this boy sassin' me?"

"So what are you and Mr. Jones into out here on this dark night, pal?" Sam asked.

"Just making a phone call," I said.

"Who you callin'? All decent folk are in bed at this hour."

"You're right," I said. "I was talking to a cop."

"You crackin' wise with me, asshole?"

I shook my head. "Used to be one myself," I said. "Just called my old boss at PCPD."

I doubted that would carry any weight with him but I threw it in just the same. Maybe we'd get hassled less if he knew I used to be on the job.

"You was a cop? So why'd you quit?"

I guess he hadn't noticed my arm yet.

"Cops," I said.

"Yeah, I heard you," he said. "Was asking why you quit being one?"

Guess I had been wrong about his intelligence being average too.

"Like I said, mostly other cops. You know the type.

68

Slow. Stupid. Abusive bullies."

"Why you—"

"Watch it, Sam," Roy yelled, "the nigger's got a gun."

Roy withdrew his weapon and pointed it at Clip, pressing Clip against the car with his forearm while pointing his pistol at Clip's head, the barrel a few inches from his good eye.

"You let your nigger carry a gun?" Sam asked me, withdrawing his gun and pointing it at me. "You packing?"

I nodded.

"Give up the heater, boy, and fast," Roy was saying, "or that car behind you's gonna have nigger brain splattered all over it."

"Ain't givin' up my gun," Clip said.

Here we go again.

"Hands up, bub," Sam said to me, his gun not far from my chest. "You only got one," he added in surprise.

"Impressive detecting," I said. "I can't understand why you haven't made captain yet."

"What's it gonna be, boy?" Roy was asking Clip in a nervous, high-pitched voice. "Surrender your rod or the rest of your life. Up to you."

So fast I wasn't sure it happened at first, Clip grabbed Roy's gun, hit him in the face with it, and had it pointing at him as he landed on the pavement.

"I thought of a third option," Clip said.

I smiled.

"Sho get tired of playin' cops and niggers all the time," Clip said.

Sam jammed the barrel of his gun into my chest.

"No way you do that to me, pal," he said. "No way."

I nodded my agreement.

"Hey, you're bleeding," he said.

"Rough night."

"You shot?"

"A while back," I said. "Keep reopening it."

He shook his head and we were quiet a moment, each of us waiting for what came next, standing still in the narrow shafts of feeble, limp light, beyond which nothing in the wide world was visible.

"What's it gonna be, soldier?" he asked. "Hole in the chest or tell the nigger to drop his gun?"

"Neither," another plainclothes cop said as he stepped out of the darkness and into our small band of light.

He was a broad, thick man. A nose that had been broken a time or two dominated a rough face beneath black hair with a slight wave in it.

"Shelby?" Sam said. "What the fuck? The nigger's got a gun. Help me."

"I'm here to help you," he said. "Help you from getting yourself killed. Or worse."

"What?"

"Take your partner and clear out. These men and I have a girl to find."

"Shelby, I don't know what the fuck's got into you tonight but the nigger assaulted Roy and I'm takin' 'em in."

"You got any idea who you're pointing that gun at?"

"Huh? Who? Just a one-armed asshole up to no good."

"His dad's the chief."

"My dad's dead," I said, and even I could hear the residue of the wounded little boy lingering in my voice.

"Stepdad," Shelby corrected.

"Chief Collins is your d—stepdad?"

I didn't answer.

"Bet he wonders just what the hell happened to you."

Chapter 12

"Who told you about Collins?" I asked.

"You mean Dad?" Dana Shelby said with a big smile.

I knew Folsom wouldn't unless he had to. He'd know how much I'd want to avoid the man and how much involving him would complicate what I was doing.

With Sam and Roy reluctantly gone, it was just the three of us now—me, Clip, and Shelby. We were standing in the empty street not far from our car.

"He did."

"He knows we're here?" I asked.

He shook his head. "While back," he said. "Came up when you crashed your car into Johnston's."

I thought about that.

I had no idea he had even known I was in town. Had he told Mom? I felt a pang of guilt for how long it had been since I'd spoken to her—even longer than normal.

We weren't close—hadn't been since Dad died. She'd lost her way in the wake of his death. She had thought Darryl Collins would help her find it again. And maybe she was right. Her decision had done me no favors, but it didn't mean it hadn't her.

"He actually had a couple of the guys keeping an eye on you when you got snatched. Lost their jobs over it."

I nodded.

Dana Shelby wasn't just broad and thick. He was squarish too, his body build resembling that of Frankenstein. His complexion was darkish and smooth, his face handsome in spite of his nose having been broken.

"Aren't exactly close, are y'all?" he said.

I smiled. "What'd he say?"

"Nothing all that bad. I just get the feeling from both of you that—"

"What'd he say?"

"Not much. Swear it. Worst thing was . . . Said you should've never been a cop to begin with. Figures that's why you lost the limb. Said he thinks you did it because of what happened to your dad."

"Did what?" I said. "What I did to get my arm blown off?"

"No," he said. "Became a cop."

"He have any insight into what vocation I'd be better suited for?"

"He did," he said with a smile. "You know him. He's got the only opinion that matters on everything."

"So what'd he say?"

"Librarian, reporter, or some sort of social worker," he said. "Way he said 'em . . . I didn't take 'em to mean . . . Didn't seem to be doing you a bad turn by sayin' 'em."

I nodded and we were quiet a moment.

He withdrew a pack of Camels from his coat pocket, shook one halfway out, and offered it to me. I shook my head. Without offering Clip one, he shook the cigarette the rest of the way out, returned the pack to his pocket, tapped it, lit it, and took a long draw from it.

"Forgot to offer Clip one," I said.

He looked genuinely surprised then apologetic.

"Sorry soldier," he said. "Didn't even think about it. He want one?"

"Ask him."

"You wanna a smoke, boy?"

Clip shook his head.

"Meant nothing by it, partner," he said. "Honest."

I nodded.

"Put you in a spot to help us without telling Collins?" I asked.

He shrugged.

"Be a problem for you if he finds out?"

"Doesn't matter," he said.

"Why's that?"

"On account of what I owe Henry Folsom," he said. "Could cost me my badge and it wouldn't matter. He's been holding a marker of mine for a while. Now he's cashing it in."

I nodded.

"Y'all are going to have to fill in a few holes for me, fellas," he said. "All I know is that you want information on the murder at Johnston's, help finding a girl that disappeared from there, and you're looking for an army nurse there the night you was."

"They were all there the night I was," I said. "The night we arrived."

"We?"

"Let's go," I said. "I'll fill you in as we have time along the way. We can't stop. Don't need to slow down."

He nodded. "Where you wanna start?"

"Whatcha got?" I asked.

"Case file on victim—Betty Jane Knox. Address on missing girl—Doris Perkins. Got a pal of mine chasing down a lead on the army nurse. He should have something for me—if there is anything to have—in just a few."

The truth was I didn't know what to do next. I just knew we were running out of time and I had to find her, had to do something. I just didn't have the time to do something wrong.

I could feel myself begin to panic inside, could feel my center threatening to break apart. What should I do? What was the best way to find her? What was the best way to proceed?

I took a deep breath and let it out slowly.

"Let's look at Betty Jane's file on the way over to Doris Perkins'," I said. "Then if the lead on the nurse pans out we'll be ready to break off and deal with it."

"You're callin' the shots," Shelby said. "So it don't matter none anyway, but not for nothing, it's what I would've said do."

Chapter 13

I was riding with Dana Shelby in his unmarked, looking at the case file.

Clip was following us in our car.

Tallahassee seemed abandoned, its sidewalks rolled up and stowed, its citizens tucked away in their beds for the night, oblivious to the deeds being done in the dark.

Shelby's cop car was so clean it seemed to never have been ridden in. I had been in squad cars with no clutter before, a few that even seemed unused in any kind of personal way, but nothing nearly this immaculate.

"How long you been assigned this car?"

"Since day one. Why?"

"How long?"

"It's a '40, so nearly three years. Why?"

"Seems new."

"Don't care for clutter."

"And not given to overstatement," I said.

He didn't seem to know how to respond, so he said, "Let me know you got any questions about the file."

I returned my attention to it.

There wasn't much in it and it didn't take long to

look over.

There was exactly nothing in the file. No suspects. No leads. No clues. No nothing.

"Elementary," I said.

"Solve it already?"

"Just stating the obvious. That it's obvious."

He shot me a raised-eyebrow look then returned his gaze to the road.

We were on Old St. Augustine Road, Florida's first highway, built in 1824 to link Pensacola and St. Augustine. The narrow, meandering two-lane cut out of the dense woods was as Old South as anything you could still see. Above us, seen in the streaks and flashes from the spill of headlights, a heavy canopy of oak and hickory formed a beautiful cover for the road, their large branches draped with thick gray curtains of Spanish moss.

"Obviously a hit," I said.

"Which begs the question. Why's a nurse at Johnston's Sanatorium get taken out by a pro?"

"Y'all have any theories on that?"

He nodded. "Yeah. All the ones in the file."

I laughed.

"Clearly we got no fuckin' clue. You?"

I nodded. "As a matter of fact I do."

"Spill it, pal. I could use some good news on this one."

"It's part of a cover-up," I said. "So's Doris being missing."

"You talking spies and intrigue and wartime conspiracy shit?"

"Not exactly. Just a powerful man covering up his crimes—something he's done his entire life."

"Whatta you say you tell me the whole story."

I did.

Well, much of it anyway.

When I was finished he said, "What is it about this girl, man? You gotta tell me."

"It's not just who she is," I said. "It's who we are together. It's like finding your best self hidden in another person. It's what home feels like after being lost at sea or left for dead in a desert. I'd had girlfriends before, had even been in love—a couple of times with great girls. The kind that make you happy and you make your wife. The very best of that is so far from this that it's like you're not even talking about the same thing."

I kept on for a while and when I finished he remained motionless and speechless, and I could tell it was out of a kind of reverence and maybe even a little longing.

It was by far one of the best reactions I'd ever received. Most people were so awkward and self-conscious or cynical and incredulous they either condescended or over-sentimentalized.

Doris lived in a red brick bungalow off Baker Street. Her car, a white DeSoto coupe, was parked in the drive.

We parked behind it.

The house and yard were dark and looked deserted—papers piled up, mail overrunning the box, Christmas decorations turned over.

Clip joined us as we approached the house on foot.

"I'a go 'round to the back," he said.

Shelby tapped on the front door, waited, then tried

it. It was unlocked.

The moment the door opened, we could hear it.

The voice was unmistakable. Edward R. Murrow reporting from Great Britain. It was coming from an RCA radio-phonograph, the model the ads had said was the last produced before they went "all out" in war work.

The dark, still house. The disembodied voice. The scene was disconcerting.

And then we found a light. And turned off the radio. And then the house was so quiet, so still, it was even more disturbing.

Nothing in the smell of the place indicated we'd find Doris dead, but the house did have that unmistakable closed-up odor of abandonment, of still stale air and lifelessness, of the slow decay of another kind.

There was very little furniture, but what there was was nice. Floral designed couch and chair, textured wallpapers—all in muted and gray-tinged pinks, greens, and blues.

We looked around a few minutes, but found nothing out of the ordinary.

"No sign of foul play," Shelby said. "Looks like she just walked out, left her car in the drive and her radio running in here."

"And didn't pack or take anything . . . except . . . Did you see her purse?"

He began looking around for it.

"Whatta you thinkin'?" he said. "She takes her purse, she just walked out, but if it's still here she was forcibly taken?"

"Not necessarily," I said. "But could point in one of those directions."

"Here it is," he said.

He had found her purse on the kitchen table partially beneath a newspaper and beside a stack of unopened mail.

"So," he said. "She was probably taken."

I nodded. "Probably."

"But without a struggle."

"Or one that was straightened back up."

"Guy takes the time to straighten up any sign of struggle but leaves the radio on?"

"Maybe," I said. "Car in the drive, radio on. Nobody knows she's not home."

"Why not leave a light on then?"

"He could've snatched her during the day," I said. "She had just come in, clicks on the radio, sits down to go through the mail, and he grabs her. Or he did leave a light on and it burned out."

Clip appeared in the back doorway.

"Hate to interrupt all the detecting you all doing," he said, "but we got company."

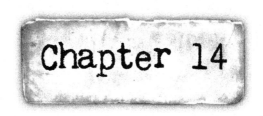

Chapter 14

"Spotted 'im when I first come up," Clip said. "Waited to see what he gonna do."

We were standing in the tiny kitchen at the very back of the house, looking out the window into the dark yard.

"And?" Shelby said.

"He not doin' nothin'. Just hiding in the bushes watching."

"Do you see him?" Shelby asked me.

I shook my head.

"He there," Clip said.

I nodded.

"Whatcha wanna do?" Clip asked me.

"Let's have a little chat with him."

"I can go out the front door and around the side and come up behind him," Clip said.

I nodded again. "Thanks."

"Give me two minutes then come out the back," he said. "Case he run back this way."

We did.

While we waited, Shelby said, "Anything bother you about all this?"

"Lots."

"I mean about the dame. Her place. Her car."

"Yeah," I said. "How's she pay for it all on a nurse's salary?"

He nodded. "No way she does. It been two minutes."

I nodded. "Let's go."

Shelby went first. As he opened the door, Clip was yelling.

We ran out, across a short concrete slab patio, and down some stone steps into the backyard.

Some of the steps were unstable, giving, shifting, rocking as our feet came down on them.

"RUNNIN'," Clip was yelling. "HE ON THE MOVE. WATCH OUT FOR THE—"

Before he could get out the last word, the ground fell out from beneath us and we were rolling down a steep incline, losing our hats along the way.

When we finally came to a stop at the bottom, and my eyes had adjusted, I could see that the house was built on a hill. The drop-off, which began just ten feet from the back wall of the house, sloped sharply down some thirty feet, a stone step staircase hollowed out in the middle of it.

"You okay?" I asked Shelby.

No response.

I pushed up on my knees as best I could. It was always difficult to balance with one arm. Scrambling over to Shelby, I could see that he was not moving.

I withdrew my lighter, snapped it open, and popped it on. There was blood just above his brow, and a rising lump. He had hit his head on one of the stone steps as we tumbled down and had been knocked unconscious.

"HERE HE COME," Clip yelled down from somewhere on top of the hill.

I looked up in time to see the man no doubt looking like I had just a few moments before. He was short and round, which seemed to help him roll better.

I stood and withdrew my weapon and when he finally came to rest at the base of the hill, I was standing over him, gun drawn, looking down the barrel of it at him.

Looking up at me, he raised his hands.

"Take it easy there, pal," he said. "Don't shoot."

He had very short arms and legs and a large, oblong torso—like an egg with limbs.

A moment later Clip made it down and lifted the little man to his feet.

"What happened to him?" the man asked, nodding at Shelby, who was moaning and beginning to stir a little.

"Hit his head," I said. "He'll be fine."

"How 'bout we aks the questions?" Clip said. "The hell you doin' here?"

"Nothing."

"What's your name?" I asked.

"Daniel Armando," he said.

"What're you doing here, Danny?"

"Daniel," he said. "Nothing. Just hanging out."

"Oh yeah?" Clip said. "So why'd you run?"

"Someone was chasing me," he said.

"What the hell happened?" Shelby said. "Help me up."

I reached down and helped him up while telling him what had happened, Clip continuing to hold Armando.

After Shelby was standing, I kept my hand on him for another moment. "You okay?"

"Yeah. I'm all right, fella. Thanks. World's just spinning a little fast for me. I'll get used to it."

In another moment, Shelby turned his attention to Armando.

"What's his story?"

"He was just hanging out," I said. "Only ran 'cause he was being chased."

"I'm being serious, fellas," Armando said. "People are disappearing and dying. There's three of y'all and y'all look like the kind of cats who make people disappear or dead. 'Specially the colored one. He looks like he'd just as soon shoot me as anything else."

"You not wrong," Clip said.

Shelby flashed his badge. "Let's have the truth," he said. "Give it a me good and maybe I won't blame you for the bump on my head."

"Y'all are cops?" Armando said.

"The hell you call me?" Clip said, bowing up and stepping toward him.

"Didn't mean you."

"Story, pal," Shelby said. "And fast."

"I'm private," he said. "On the job. Looking for the girl that lives here. Watching the house when you three showed up and started chasing me."

"You been watching the house and you didn't know the hill was here?" I asked.

"No, I knew," he said. "I didn't fall. The nigger pushed me."

I looked at Clip.

"The nigger did indeed," he said, his smile lighting up the night.

"My license is in my coat pocket," Armando said.

"I've got a rod in a holster on my right hip."

"No you don't," Clip said. "Haven't for some time now. The nigger lifted it just 'fore he humpty-dumptied your eggheaded ass down the hill."

Clip was right. He was eggheaded. I hadn't really noticed. It was as if his head were a small egg balanced atop the larger egg of his body.

He reached down and felt his empty holster, then nodded in appreciation.

Shelby reached into his coat pocket and withdrew his license.

"See?" Armando said. "And I've got a friend or two on the force. You can call 'em."

"I can?" Shelby said. "Gee thanks, fella. You're a swell guy, all generous and what not."

He studied the license a little longer.

"Well?" I asked.

"License is legit," he said.

He looked back at Armando. "Who're your friends on the force?"

"Harold Patterson and Don April."

"What's Don's wife's name?"

"He doesn't have one, but Harold does. Her name is Pat. Pat Patterson. She hates it, but she loves Harold so much she really don't mind."

Shelby nodded at me and returned the license to Armando.

"So," I said, "who're you looking for?"

"Dame that lives in the house up there," he said. "Doris Perkins."

"Who hired you to find her?"

"Can't tell you that, cat," he said. "Sorry."

Shelby said, "Well, as long as you're sorry. We understand."

He then slapped the man across the face hard and openhanded, and the report was loud in the stillness and darkness.

"What the hell—"

"Listen to me you fat little fuck," Shelby said. "I'm in no mood. You answer our goddamn questions and you answer them the moment we ask them or I will fuck you up but good then arrest you for making me do it. Understand?"

He stopped rubbing his cheek long enough to nod.

"Who hired you?" Shelby asked.

"Girl's brother. Black market kingpin named Lee Perkins. She doesn't have anything to do with him, but she'll take some of his ill-gotten gains."

"Evidently so will you," Shelby said.

Armando laughed. "Guess so. Anyway, he thinks he's big and bad enough that nobody should mess with his little sister. But he can't be totally sure she didn't just disappear to get away from him."

Shelby looked at me. "I've heard of this guy. Runs the black market in this region. Makes money on the war. Shortages. Rations. There's nothing not available for the right price."

"Maybe I should talk to him 'bout gettin' my eye back," Clip said.

Chapter 15

"What if she did just walk away?" I asked.

We were back in the house, having gathered our hats from the side of the hill, cleaning up and using the phone.

All four of us were in the small kitchen. Shelby had his head under the tap, letting the water run over the spot where the rock got him. Clip still stood close to Daniel Armando, but wasn't touching him any longer. I was leaning on one side of the doorway, the tumble down the hill having done the wound in my abdomen no good at all.

"Huh?" Shelby said from beneath the tap.

"What if she did just walk away?" I said again. "What if she's just hiding from her brother. Or what if her disappearance has something to do with him? What if it has nothing to do with Lauren?"

"Be hell of a coincidence," Clip said.

I nodded.

"Yeah," Shelby said. "The timing would be—

"Lauren doesn't have time for me to make a wrong decision," I said, my stress-constricted words coming out strained and too fast. "I can't go very far down a wrong path without it costing her her life. Am thinking maybe we should just follow up on the army nurse instead."

I could feel the panic creeping back in, fear gripping my heart, constricting my viscera, affecting my ability to move, make a decision, think, act.

I can't kill her again. I can't.

"And you go up against a guy like Perkins," Armando said, "you better be sure. Why risk getting killed if you have other lines of inquiry to follow up on?"

Clip laughed. "Lines of inquiry," he repeated, shaking his head.

Shelby finished rinsing his head and dried it on a dishtowel on the tile countertop next to the sink. He turned toward me, still toweling his hair.

"It's your call," he said. "I'll go with whatever you decide."

I looked over at Clip, imploring him to tell me what to do, to help me make a decision Lauren could live with.

Our eyes locked, his one eye narrowing, his gaze intensifying, holding. Lowering his head slightly and raising his eyebrows, he was able to communicate both concern and a settling support.

"Nothin' to decide 'til we know where nurse whatshername is—or even might be."

"Powell," I said, nodding. "Valerie Powell."

"Let him call in," he said. "See if the lead played out. Gots no decision 'til then."

I nodded. "Thank you."

"I'll make the call," Shelby said.

While he did, Clip and I took turns cleaning up under and drinking from the tap, alternating watching Armando.

"Say, can I get my gat back?" Armando asked me.

"I don't have it," I said. "Why you asking me?"

"He think you my massa," Clip said.

"Look pal, I didn't mean no offense. I just thought the soldier was in charge. My mistake."

Clip unloaded the revolver, pocketed the rounds, and handed Armando the weapon.

"It's not so good without those," he said, nodding toward Clip's pocket.

"Just stay close to us," Clip said. "We protect you."

Armando started to say something but Clip cut him off.

"Mean, if'n he say I can," he said, nodding toward me.

"Cute," he said. "Protection and entertainment. What's next? You gonna feed me too?"

Shelby returned to the room and shrugged.

"Not sure," he said. "She may be at this little frolic pad down off Gains, but . . . I don't know . . . Picture I'm gettin' of her . . . she seems too hinky for it."

I nodded.

"Your call," he said.

"See?" Armando said to Clip. "He's in charge. Give me my bullets back."

"I'm gonna check in with Henry Folsom while we're at a phone," I said. "Then I'll decide what to do next."

"We may be gettin' close, Jimmy," Henry Folsom said.

"To Lauren?"

"Had a car turn around before one of our roadblocks," he said. "One of the descriptions sounded like

De Grasse. He got away, but I've got patrol cars searching the area where he was last seen. I really think it's him."

I thought about it.

I felt funny calling long distance on Doris Perkins's phone, but had to reach Folsom while I had the chance. I guess I could've reversed the charges, but it hadn't occurred to me until this moment.

"You still there?" he asked.

"Yeah. Just thinking about De Grasse. They know to take him alive, right?"

"Strict orders from me," he said. "You and I are going to be able to have a nice little conversation with him. I guarantee it."

My heart grew heavier, its thudding beats seeming to come from within my stomach now.

I was okay about things until he guaranteed it.

"How are things going over there?" he asked.

I told him.

"Sounds promising," he said when I finished. "Just watch yourself with Lee Perkins. He's a truly dangerous man. Make sure Clip and Dana know too and y'all look out for each other. Be very vigilant."

"Will do."

"I think finding Valerie Powell or whatever her name is is key. I hope the lead pans out. I'm still trying to dig up info on her from here. Let me know what happens."

I started to say something, but he continued.

"And Jimmy, we will find her. Lauren I mean. I won't stop until I do."

"Thanks."

"I'm . . ." he began, and then stopped. "I just want you to know that everything's going to be okay. I'm gonna make sure of it."

I thought about what he might be trying to say.

"Okay," I said.

"I just want you to know that this isn't all on you alone," he said. "I'm . . . I won't stop. No matter what."

"You trying to say that if something happens to me you'll carry on the search and won't stop until you find her, and will take care of her after you do?"

"Well, yes. I guess I am."

"Never thought anything but," I said. "Thank you."

"That, and . . ."

I waited a long time.

Finally, he said, "Sorry. Losing Gladys has me messed up. I . . . I just . . . Just promise me you'll be careful. People like Perkins . . . Just take good care of yourself, son."

"What's the plan, boss man?" Shelby asked when I walked into the small living room where they were sitting.

"Daniel here will introduce me and Clip to Lee Perkins while you chase down the lead on Valerie Powell. That way you don't scare Perkins off by throwing cops at him and we don't miss the angel of death if she's really there."

"Sounds good," Shelby said.

"Yeah," Armando said, "all but the part about me introducing you to Mr. Perkins. That ain't gonna happen."

Clip let out a low, mean, humorless laugh. "Oh it gonna happen. You can bet money your ass can't afford to lose on it. It that sure a thang."

Chapter 16

Lee Perkins lived in one of the one hundred fifty rooms in the Floridan Hotel on the corner of Monroe and Call across from St. John's Episcopal Church. He was a small man with dark, dead eyes, a dry wit, and deliberate manner.

Since the Floridan, which proclaimed itself as "North Florida's most successful hotel," was "whites only," Clip and I couldn't stay here, but because of Perkins's pull, we were allowed to meet him in the empty Cypress Lounge, where at other times politicians met to discuss legislation.

"I should have you bumped off just for disturbing my beauty sleep," he said.

It wasn't late. Not quite ten o'clock yet. And it was funny to think of a gangster who ruled the black market underworld going to bed early.

He was in silk pajamas, house slippers, and a robe, the belt cinched tight around his narrow midsection.

"And you," he said to Armando. "Suppose you tell me what I should do with you?"

His voice was low and flat, monotone and menacing.

"Mr. Perkins, they gave me no choice."

"Little man, you always have a choice. Always."

Perkins was the only man I'd seen in a while who was actually smaller than Armando, and it was funny to hear him call him little man.

"They're looking for your sister too," he said. "They broke into her house. I knew you'd know what to do."

"You take chances, don't you?" he said.

"I'm sorry, Mr. Perkins," he said. "Honest I am."

It was an act, but Perkins didn't seem to know it. Maybe this was the only side of Armando he'd ever seen.

"Skip it."

"I really am sorry, Mr. Perkins. It won't happen again."

"I said forget it."

"Okay sir. Thank you, sir."

Perkins looked at me. It was like looking into a dead man's eyes. They were flat, opaque, lifeless, dim windows to nothing, no soul, nothing human.

"You're looking for my sister," he said. "Wanna tell me why?"

I did.

"You think her disappearance is connected to this Lewis dame who may have died or disappeared herself?"

"I do."

"That's why I brought him," Armando said. "I knew you'd want to know about the connection."

Following Perkins's lead, Armando was ignoring Clip again.

Perkins studied me for a long moment.

Being here alone with us, unarmed, in his pajamas no less, demonstrated how little threat he perceived us to pose, but even more so just how very invulnerable he felt.

He wasn't just a hard hood. He was powerful. And

fearless. He didn't hide from anything or anyone. He didn't hide behind anyone or anything either.

"Daniel," Perkins said, "you and the nigger wait outside."

"Of the room, Mr. Perkins?"

"Of the hotel," he said.

Clip looked at me.

I frowned but nodded.

He turned and walked out without waiting for Armando.

"You sure, Mr. Perkins?"

"You just keep taking chances, don't you, fella. In the street, now."

"I'll be right out there if you need me, Mr. Perkins."

"Sure, guy," he said with a self-amused smile. "I can't handle the one-armed wounded soldier who forced you to bring him here in the first place, you'll be the first person I call."

When Armando was gone, Perkins stood, walked over behind the bar, and began to mix himself a drink.

As he did, I thought about how most of us in the country were suffering, sacrificing for the war, but not Lee Perkins and those like him. They were actually turning a profit, living better than ever before.

I knew his kind. In an earlier era, he'd have been a ridge runner, a bootlegger, a moonshiner. Before that, he'd have run guns. Before that, who knows, but it would've been on the backs of others, of decent people who couldn't begin to guess at the depth of cruelty and lack of humanity in the dark void at the center of someone like Perkins.

For a little over a month now, rationed items

included bicycles, fuel oil, stoves, shoes, meat, lard, shortening and oils, cheese, butter, margarine, processed foods, dried fruits, canned milk, firewood, coal, jams, jellies, and fruit butter. OPA, the federal Office of Price Administration, had also set limits on the number of gallons of gasoline we could buy each week.

Most of us, most everyone I knew, willingly, even gladly, gave, saved, helped. Over a year and a half ago now every man, woman, and child had been issued a ration book filled with coupons that limited the amounts of meat, sugar, canned goods, and other food we could buy each week. But not people like Perkins—not those who had the money to buy black market and who didn't have the character not to, and not the criminals who supplied their demand.

When he finished fixing his drink, he rejoined me back at the table.

"Do you know who I am?" he asked.

"I do."

"And yet you get me out of bed in the night in this disrespectful manner. Why?"

"No time to do it any other way," I said. "And . . ."

"And?"

"And I couldn't've guessed you'd be in bed this early."

He smiled. "All decent people are," he said. "Bit player like you wouldn't be, wouldn't understand."

I nodded. He was probably right.

"And?" he said.

"And?" I asked.

"There is more."

"And I'd do anything to find the woman I'm looking

for."

"Anything?" he said. "That is interesting. Many a man tosses that around—anything. I believe it may actually be true of you. No way to know for certain until . . . until you get a certain test. But there is more."

"More?"

"Yes. More."

"Then I must not know what it is," I said.

"You are not afraid."

"That's not true," I said.

"I know afraid," he said. "I deal with it every day. You are not afraid."

"I am afraid," I said. "I will not let it stop me."

"If a man's fear does not control him, can that man be said to be afraid?"

"Maybe not," I said.

"You interest me," he said. "You're in a hard man's game, but I'm not so sure you're a hard man."

"A cop told me something like that earlier tonight."

He nodded. "The day you have Lee Perkins and a cop telling you the same thing, you listen."

I shrugged.

"What?"

"Doesn't matter," I said. "Nothing for it."

"All right, fella," he said. "That may be."

"And I might be harder than you think."

"Oh, I think you're plenty hard," he said. "I just wonder how deep it goes."

I nodded. "I'm sure I'll find out soon enough."

"Undoubtedly. Like to be there when you do."

"Maybe you will be."

We were silent a moment, but I didn't let myself

think about what he had said. I couldn't.

"I can help you with your girl, soldier," he said. "But you have to do something for me."

"What's that?"

"Tell me why a woman is worth all this," he said. "I've never loved a woman like that. Explain it to me, fella, and I'll help you out."

"I'd had women before Lauren," I said. "I'd even loved one or two. They were pretty and pretty smart. At least one of them was near perfect. None of them was Lauren. None of them made me know not just that I'd gladly give up every other woman in the world but that I had to. The thing is you don't know what you don't have—not until you have it. Then you can never not know it again. I might have settled for pretty good or may even have been one of the lucky stiffs that finds close to perfect, maybe even very close, but once Lauren came into my life, close enough—no matter how close it was—never would be again. I've lost her not once but twice. If she's alive, I'm going to find her and I'm not going to lose her again."

He nodded and seemed to think about it for a moment.

"Ever feel like a sap?"

"Sure, but not about Lauren, not anymore. Not for the way I love her."

He nodded again, and again sat there in silence seeming to ponder what I had said.

"I hired the peeper to watch the house for two reasons," he said at length. "To see who comes there looking for her."

"And?"

"To keep up the illusion that I don't know where she

is."

"You have her?" I said, my voice and brows rising.

He nodded. "You do anything with anything I share with you against me or my sister and I'll have you killed."

"Why?"

"Do you understand?" he said.

I nodded.

"I can kill you or have you killed before you leave this room," he said. "Do you understand?"

I nodded again.

"This thing that happened with your girl, it frightened Doris. She talked to me about it. I began to look into it a bit. When the other nurse was killed, it scared her enough to ask for my protection—not an easy thing for her to do."

"So she's okay?"

"She's in a room up above us in this very hotel, sleeping like an innocent."

"And Lauren?"

"I've been looking into the whole thing," he said. "Someone poses a threat to my sister, I'm gonna find out who and put him down hard. Understand?"

"I do."

"I don't know much yet and I'll tell you why. It's early days into my inquiry and since Doris is safe, I have not had to pursue this thing with the, ah, intensity or speed I would have normally, which is good because I've had a number of issues in my business that required my attention. But here's what I got—and I'm not going to stop just because you'll now be following the same leads, so stay out of my way and let me know what you uncover, understand?"

I nodded.

"I don't know if your girl's still alive, soldier," he said, "but I know who knows for sure. Woman named Vanessa Patrick. She showed up that night using the name Valerie Powell and took your girl away from Doris and Betty Jane. Don't know if it was to kill her or steal her, but either way she's the doer."

"You sure about the name?"

He nodded. "Why?"

"Pal of mine is over at the Panther Room looking for Valerie Powell right now."

"It's no good. Her real name is Patrick. She's got a room at the Cactus Motel. She ain't the sort of dame that'd be at the Panther."

Chapter 17

The Panther Room was a low rent club in an old brick building off Gaines, with a bar and a bandstand and not much else. When the joint was filled with BYTs and hep cats and kittens all dolled up and togged out dragging their hoofs, it seemed like a decent enough place, but when it was empty you could see just what a dive it really was.

By the time we arrived, the parking lot beneath the big red-and-orange neon sign that read The Panther Room, the letters stacked atop one another, was filled with patrol cars and a paddy wagon.

I had taken the time to go with Lee up to his sister's room to verify she was really there—of her own free will—and so had not gotten here quite as quickly as I might have.

We parked across the street and walked over.

The lot had been cordoned off, patrolmen posted in intervals of about twenty feet.

"What's going on?" I asked the first one we came to.

"Police stuff, or ain't it obvious?"

He was a pale, blond, big-headed kid with a big round belly, his hand on his baton.

"What happened?"

"What's the idea, pal? I just told you. Better breeze before I bust you one."

"I just need to know if—"

"Look soldier, I been polite on account of your service to our country and all, but you really don't listen so good. Now, blow or I'm gonna get mad and it'll cost you plenty."

"I'm here to see Detective Dana Shelby," I said. "Whatta you say you grab him for me?"

"LIEUTENANT," he yelled back over his shoulder without taking his gaze off me. "LIEUTENANT."

"WHAT IS IT, MORRIS?" someone yelled back from the huddle of cops gathered around what must be a body on the ground.

"FELLA HERE LOOKING FOR SHELBY."

My heart dropped at that.

"OH YEAH? BE RIGHT THERE."

"Where's Shelby?" I asked.

"Lieutenant'll be here in a minute."

The cops from earlier in the evening, Average Sam and Tall Roy, spotted us and walked over.

"You two," Sam said. "Should've known."

"Hiya boys," I said. "Whatta you say you tell us what's going on?"

"Suppose you tell us, bub," Sam said. "Whatta you know about this?"

"Don't even know what *this* is," I said. "Why I'm asking."

Roy shook his head. "Just keep taking chances, fella. We don't mind."

Sam said, "Level with us, pal. Chief's son or not. Don't matter. You ain't playin' me for a sap no more. Not with one of ours on the ground."

"Shelby?" I asked.

"Like you don't know."

"I don't," I said, "but I do know why he was here, what he was—"

"James?"

I had an instant and intense visceral reaction to the voice. The sound carried within its vibrations the loss of a father, the weakness of a mother, the rigidity of a stepdad drill instructor, the bullying that bordered on abuse, the anger, the guilt, the grief, and ultimately the relief and release of manhood.

I turned to see Darryl Collins, Chief of Police.

"Chief," I said.

"What're you doing here?"

"He was just about to tell us," Sam said.

"You mixed up in this?" he asked me.

"Can we talk?" I said.

"We pulled them over earlier tonight, Chief," Sam said. "Shelby called us off of 'em. He was with them last time we saw him."

"Thank you, Samuel," he said. "I've got it from here. Go back to what you were doing."

"Yes sir."

"Come with me," Collins said to me.

I motioned for Clip to come and we ducked under the rope.

"He with you?" Collins asked.

I nodded.

He shook his head in disapproval. "Okay. Come on."

He took us several feet inside the perimeter to an empty area where we'd have privacy. There were a few cops scattered throughout the lot, but mostly they were all clumped in the front corner near the building and, I assumed, the body.

"I'm Chief Collins," he said to Clip.

"This is Clipper Jones of the Ninety-ninth Fighter Squadron First Tactical Unit."

"Presently?"

"Nah suh, presently I of the Riley Detective Agency."

Collins let out a mean little laugh at that.

Turning back to me, he said, "Whatta you say you tell me what you know."

I did. Nearly all of it.

When I finished he was quiet for a long moment.

Beneath the neon light, the pavement of the mostly empty lot looked bathed in blood, its red residue forming a film on everything.

The intermittent flash of the squad cars added to the tension and intensity of the scene, the brilliance on the black backdrop of dark night making it seem later than it really was.

"You got one of my men killed," he said. "The facts support no other possible conclusion, leave no room for any other interpretation."

After all this time his disappointment and disapproval was still a knife slice through a sweet spot of skin and muscle and scar tissue—the latter caused by him many years before.

"Whatta you say we see what happened before we draw any conclusions?"

He waved his arm in a be-my-guest gesture toward to the clump of cops, and we walked over toward them.

"Whatcha got, Staney?" he asked as we walked up.

"It's Dana Shelby, Chief," Staney said. "They got one of ours."

I was gripped by a vice-like guilt that began to buckle my knees.

I looked down to see Shelby as I tried to steady myself. He was lying face up on the ground not far from the open door of his car, his bullet-riddled body contorted slightly, his right foot bent back beneath him.

"It was an ambush, sir," he said. "Witnesses say they started firing the moment he opened the door. They shot the shit out of him and the car."

"Language, Lieutenant."

"Sorry sir. He didn't even draw his weapon. Two men unloaded into him and his car, then jumped back into their vehicle and sped away. Nobody can give us much to go on—on the shooters or their car."

Collins looked over at me, his narrowed eyes burning with anger and disgust.

"You got a good cop killed," he said.

The other officers standing around all suddenly turned the focus of their attention onto me.

Everything went silent and still, the only sound the soft whine of the cold wind and the hum and flicker of the neon sign hanging above us.

"Who was he here to meet?" he asked.

"He thought he was meeting Valerie Powell," I said, "but that's not her real name."

"What's her real name?"

"Vanessa Patrick."

"Wilson," Collins said to one of the cops nearby, "see if there's a Valerie Powell or a Vanessa Patrick in there."

Wilson turned to walk inside.

"And don't just go by the witness statements or the names they've given. Check IDs."

"Yes sir."

"Why'd y'all think she was here?"

I shrugged. "Not sure. He had someone in the department working on it for him. He made a call. He was told she might be here, but he said he didn't think so. Said he suspected the place was too low-class for her."

Collins looked back at his men. "Who was working with Dana on this?"

No one responded.

"Well, find out," he said. "Now. And find me an address for Valerie Powell and Vanessa Patrick."

I considered telling him about Lee Perkins and what he'd said about Patrick having a room at the Cactus, but decided I couldn't run the risk of their involvement getting in the way of me finding Lauren.

"No Powell or Patrick here, Chief," Wilson said when he came back outside.

"You sure?"

"Positive."

"Wouldn't be if it was just a straight setup," Clip said.

Everyone turned to look at him with the awe of superstitious people believing they've just witnessed a miracle.

"Speaking's not the only trick he does," I said.

"Wouldn't need her here for an ambush," Clip continued. "Not even a fake her."

"The nigger's right," someone in the group

mumbled.

Collins looked down at Shelby and shook his head. "Just can't believe he's dead."

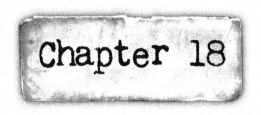

Chapter 18

The Cactus was a roadside motel out on US 90 that looked to have about fourteen rooms.

About as basic as a block-building motel could get, there was nothing nice or fancy about it. So why had both Shelby and Perkins said Powell/Patrick seemed too well-to-do a lady for a place like the Panther Room?

Perhaps she was only staying here because there were no other rooms available in town right now.

Florida had 328,934 hotel rooms not being used by the service for the war, and the Florida Chamber of Commerce encouraged tourists to come take advantage of them. And come they did. It was counterintuitive but we had more visitors to our state just now than we did before the war started.

Florida was booming—and not just from all the federal contracts for war production, but from the money it put in people's pockets and from the tourists we were attracting. Today alone, the Hialeah Racetrack took in $600,000 in bets, while the state's dog tracks took in $100,000. And today was no special day. It was like all the others this season in the Sunshine State.

Hotels owners could charge full price for rooms not being used by the service. Many of them received even more in under-the-table sweeteners for vacancies—something the Office of Price Administration and Office of Rent Control seemed to be able to do little about.

I was sure Vanessa Patrick couldn't afford to do something like that.

According to the night clerk she could no longer even afford a room at the Cactus.

"Spent her last dollar on a bus ticket back to Birmingham," he said.

He was a tall, odd-looking fellow—youngish, but didn't look it because he was balding and his heavily lined skin seemed to lack nearly all elasticity.

"Spent most of the ones before that one on a fella," he said. "No, it's not what you're thinking. She actually hired this guy to look after her—you know, like a bodyguard. I don't know how she could afford it as long as she did. But it always catches up with you. All good things, you know?"

"Why'd she have a bodyguard and for how long?"

"Gee mister, I can't rightly recall how long, but not too. It was a recent thing."

"Do you know why she hired one in the first place?"

"No idea," he said. "Like I said, she didn't do it for long. Maybe she didn't even need one at all. I never saw that anyone bothered her. Probably just being dramatic. Delusions of grandeur. You know what they say—they're as mad as a box of snakes."

"Who is?" I asked.

"Actresses."

"When'd she leave?" I asked.

He seemed to think about it. "I'd say little over an hour ago. Where're y'all going? Didn't you want to see her room?"

We found Vanessa Patrick in the Blue Line Cafe in Union Bus Station, at a booth in the back waiting for a bus that wouldn't come until early the next morning.

I sat across from her in the booth. Clip turned a chair around from a nearby table and sat at the end, blocking her in.

If she recognized me she gave no indication. If our sudden presence in her booth alarmed she didn't let it show.

We were the only people in the place besides two waitresses in white uniforms—one behind the counter, the other sitting wearily at a table in the front sipping coffee and nibbling toast.

The waitress behind the counter cleared her throat. "Colored section is over there," she said, jerking her head toward a single table in the front corner opposite the other waitress.

"Police business," I said. "We'll only be a moment."

"Police?" Vanessa Patrick said, looking a little relieved—something quickly undercut by doubt. "You aren't really, are you? Who sent you?"

"Somebody looking for you?" I asked. "That why you're leaving town?"

She was different than I had imagined—not stout as Bernice had said, and I wondered if that had been part of her costume or simply because she was big breasted.

She was pale as hell, as Bernice had put it, but attractive, with only a smattering of light pink freckles and strawberry blond hair that was both thick and shiny. She was also a good deal younger than I had pictured.

"Who are you, mister, really?"

"You don't recognize me?"

She studied me. "Should I?"

I shook my head.

She leaned up slightly and looked around the room.

"Whatcha looking for?" Clip asked.

She shook her head and leaned back.

"What gives, fellas?" she said, looking from me to Clip and back to me. "Is my number up? This the end of the line for me?"

"Why would it be?"

"So it's not . . ."

"You an actress?" I said.

"Why? You want an autograph?"

"Any good?" Clip asked.

"She fooled a real nurse into thinking she was one," I said.

A flash of recognition flared in her eyes then vanished.

It was only a little past eleven, but it seemed later, as if days and not hours has passed since Clip and I had first gotten in the car to head over here earlier in the evening.

Outside the diner the night was dark. No moon. No stars. No streetlamps. No lights from passing cars. Inside, it was so bright it turned the windows into mirrors. The front of the diner was only a reflection of what was inside the diner itself, as if it was a two-way mirror in an interrogation room.

I felt exposed and on display.

"Where is Lauren Lewis?" I asked.

"Who?"

"Don't," I said. "We've got you. There's only one play. Be smart and you can be on your bus when it gets here. All I want is the girl."

"And if she's dead and I had something to do with it?"

"Is she?" I said. "Did you?"

"I had no idea what I was getting mixed up in, mister," she said. "Swear I didn't. It was just a job. I was just playing a part."

"Tell me everything."

"Get in there and get her out," she said. "That's all I was hired to do and all I did. Who has you looking for her?"

"I'm not doing this for someone else," I said. "I was with her. We arrived together. She's my . . . they haven't made up a word big enough, strong enough, good enough for what she is to me."

"Oh."

"Where is she?"

"I don't know. I swear it. They had me go in, isolate her, sedate her, say she died, and wait for the coroner. They came and got her."

"Who did?"

"The coroner," she said. "The guys pretending to be the coroner. They took her away."

"Who were they?"

"No idea. Had never seen them before. Haven't seen them since. Maybe actors like me. Poor dumb bastards that owe the wrong people. It's the last I saw of her too. I swear it. I filled out the death certificate and got out of there. Never went back. These are very powerful people. Cruel. They collect debts like chits and hold onto them until they can use you and then . . ."

"Who is? Who hired you?"

"I'm real sorry about your girl, mister. Honest I am, but I've told you my part in it. That's all I did. That's all I know. I swear it."

"It's not all you know. Who hired you? Who helped you at the hospital?"

"Betty Jane Knox," she said. "She owed the wrong people same as me. She made a call. I got a call. When I got there and told her, that other nurse, and that negro nurse I'd take it from there, she's the one who convinced the others to back off." She paused. "Lauren was burned real bad."

"You mean her scars?"

"Yeah. Think Betty used them to convince the other nurse that she was army or something—that she wasn't just an ordinary patient. And remember, it was pure chaos in there. The doctor was already in surgery with you. There was a car inside the building. Rubble. Whatever she told them . . . wouldn't have been too hard to convince them of anything."

"Were you at the Panther Room earlier tonight?" I asked.

"The what?"

"You saying you don't even know what it is?"

"Yeah. And the only thing I did earlier tonight was pack and check out of my room at the Cactus."

"So who were you into and for what?" I asked.

"Huh?"

"Who'd you owe? Who hired you?"

"Mister, my life ain't been so easy. I've been through some things. Made more than my share of mistakes. The things I've seen . . . I know true cruelty. I've looked in its eyes, felt its punch. These men enjoy other people's pain. I'm leaving the area to get away from them, but I know evil's everywhere. I know I can't outrun it. But I'm gonna run as far and fast and for as long as I can."

"You're not going anywhere until you tell us who you did all this for," I said.

She laughed. "I told you, soldier," she said. "I know true cruelty. And you're not it."

"We do all right," Clip said.

She glanced over at him then back at me.

"Look at me," I said. "Look into my eyes. Do you really think I won't do absolutely anything I have to to find her?"

She held my eyes, but didn't respond.

"Harry Lewis," I said.

She nodded.

"Flaxon De Grasse."

She nodded.

"Who else?"

"I'm curious," she said. "Where do you think I was when they tapped me for this?"

I shrugged, realizing I hadn't even thought about it.

"In jail," she said. "There's no cruelty like that of a cruel cop."

Chapter 19

"Who's jail? Which cop?" I asked.

She shook her head. "I've already said far more than I meant to. Please, let's leave it at that."

"You know I can't do that," I said.

"'Fraid you gonna have to," a compact spark plug of a man with a bad crew cut said.

He had a gun in each hand. He jammed the one in his left fist into the back of Clip's head and the one in his right fist just behind my left ear.

"Hey," the waitress behind the counter said.

"Don't move," he said to her. "Don't do anything. Everybody just freeze right where you are. We're about to walk out of here and you'll never see us again, so don't do nothin' stupid."

Both waitresses held their hands up then froze in place.

His ill-fitting suit was too long for his thick, squat build, and he looked like a casual man at a funeral in borrowed dress-up clothes. He wore no hat and his oblong head was too big for his body.

"Sorry that took so long, Miss Patrick," he said.

He spoke slowly and simply, and had a certain innocence, even naiveté about him.

"It's okay, Rob," she said.

"Gots to admit," Clip said to me. "I's doubtful about her having a actual bodyguard after seeing the Cactus. Figured the night clerk was confusing one of her men friends or somethin'."

I nodded. "Thought the same thing."

"How bad they bother you while I was gone?" Rob asked.

"They're okay, Rob. Really they are. I just need to fade and you need to make sure they let me."

She spoke to him slowly and sweetly, but with no discernible condescension, treating him the way one would a loved child.

"Sure thing, Miss Patrick. I was thinkin', why don't I just drive you? I don't mind."

"Would you Rob?" she said. "That's a swell idea. You really wouldn't mind?"

"Not at all."

"Just give me a name," I said.

"Look mister, I'm sorry about your girl. Honest I am. And I wish I had never had any part of it, but I didn't have a choice and I don't know where she is. Truth is I don't know anything, and everything I told you was just me stallin' 'til Rob got back. So whatta you say you forget everything I've said and you all let us leave without Rob having to do anything to your heads that can't be undone?"

At that Rob flicked my ear with the barrel of his gun.

"So," he said. "Let the lady out of the booth and let us take a little walk."

Clip cut his eye over at me.

I gave a slight nod.

He slid his chair back slightly to let Vanessa slide out, which she did.

"Good so far," he said. "So far so good. Now take your heaters out and put them on the table. Nice and slow like."

"Ain't givin' up my gun," Clip said.

Here we go again.

"Just go," I said to Rob. "Walk out of here. We're letting you."

"Oh, you're letting me?" he said with a simpleton's laugh. "Hear that, Miss Patrick? Got a gun on each of 'em but they're letting us—"

Before he could finish, Clip was up and holding the gun that had been pointed at him, and I, still seated, had knocked the other one to the floor—which was the best I could manage given my particular limitations.

Not sure quite what to do, Rob stood there in stunned silence a moment, a slack-jawed mask of confusion on his misshapen mug.

And then it exploded.

Glass shattering.

Shards raining.

Machine gun spray.

Rounds ricocheting. Hundreds.

Extremely loud.

Blood-splattered waitress uniform. Rorschach in red on bright white cotton.

Rob crumpled onto the floor, Vanessa collapsed on top of him.

Find cover. Get gun. Return fire. Help Clip.

Clip crouching on the floor, yanking me down, firing back.

One waitress still alive. Screaming.

Reaching for gun.

Movement in periphery. Downward motion.

Turning. Too late. Hit. Hard. Knocked. Jarred. Then . . .

Adrift. Black wave. Overtaken. Darkness. Drowning. Nothing.

Chapter 20

The moon was big and bright, the night clear and cool, the river refreshing and romantic.

It was one of those rarest of times that Lauren and I actually got to spend the entire night together, and we were swimming naked in the Apalachicola River behind Ray Parker's fish camp where we were staying.

We were treading water at the end of a short, narrow dock, one arm on the ladder, the other around each other. Though high in the starless sky, the moon still shown brightly on the water, its beam bouncing like rollicking raindrops on the gently undulating ripples of the river.

"I can die happy now," she said. "I've had the big love."

"Well try to live a little longer, sister, 'cause you're gonna get it again in just a few more minutes."

"Jimmy," she said with a smile as she punched me in the chest, splashing water up into my face. "I didn't mean that. I meant—"

"I know what you meant," I said.

"I just never thought it possible," she said. "Honest

I didn't. I was content to just exist—or was until I met you. There was no way for me to know what I was missing. How can you know what you don't know? How can you even hope to imagine anything with absolutely no frame of reference? I didn't even know enough to know to want this. Now I'll never want anything else."

"I found you," I said.

I still couldn't believe I actually had.

"Yes you did. Maybe we even found each other."

I nodded.

"Truth is," she said, "love found us both. Found us for one another."

I pulled her to me, wrapping my left arm around her, not knowing then that one day it would be the only arm I'd ever get to hold her with again. With my right I continued holding the dock.

Letting go of the piling, she held me with both arms, wrapping her legs around me, clinging to me as if to save her life when actually she was saving mine.

The dark, deep river water was no longer cold on my skin, and not just because I had grown accustomed to the temperature.

She grabbed the back of my neck with her hand and pulled me into a hard, wet, passionate kiss that sent pure, primal, preternatural energy arcing through me.

After a while, when we separated ever so slightly, we bobbed breathlessly, our eyes fixed on the other's, something ineffable, ephemeral, indescribable passing between us.

"Whatta we gonna do?" I asked.

"About?"

"This. Us. I can't keep getting so little of you, of

this. Can't keep sharing you."

"You're not sharing me," she said. "We'll figure it out. I promise."

"But—"

"Baby, listen, I know how you feel. I feel the same way. But we've got to trust. Love found us. Love will look after us. If we'll let her. I don't want to waste a second of our time together worrying about future times. Okay?"

I nodded.

"When something is this good, this ideal, this magical, this . . . unparalleled . . . it's only natural to want more, but worrying how to get it robs us of what we have now. And we can't let that happen."

We made love on a blanket on the dock beneath the moon, our bodies damp with drops of river water that had traveled an infinite distance to join in our joining.

Her burned body was an ancient charr-scarred scroll filled with the most beautiful words ever penned, a surviving codex containing the secrets of existence, the meaning of life and love and of all things.

Our bodies were for each other complimentary puzzle pieces, cut with precision, fitting with perfection. We were made for each other, our very beings joining and responding in ways that before now I had believed were hyperbole, the stuff of misguided myth and romance literature.

There was no sound in heaven or on earth as sweet as that of my name in her mouth when we made love, when said as a plea and a prayer, when breathed as a revelation and an ecstatic utterance.

When our lovemaking was momentarily complete and our bodies, with a different kind of dampness on them, were entwined beneath the blanket, we alternated between gazing up at the moon and into each other's eyes.

"You know what this is," she said. A statement, not a question.

I didn't respond. I knew she wouldn't wait for me to before telling me what this was.

"This is what the mystics meditate on," she said. "What the ecstatic go on about. This. Us. What we're experiencing. What we have is what the devout are looking for."

And though later I would lose it, would lose her, and therefore my way entire, in that moment I knew the truth of what she was saying with the certainty of a saint.

But before I could respond, a hand reached up from the dark waters of the river, clutched her ankle, and pulled her in.

There was nothing I could do to stop it from happening. I held on to her, clung to her as if to life itself, but I couldn't keep her, couldn't prevent what was happening.

And then she disappeared down into the deep, dark, mysterious river that a moment before had been for both of us womblike in its warm embrace.

Chapter 21

"Jimmy? Jimmy."

I opened my eyes to see the kind, soft, aging, but still beautiful, face of my mother.

"Jimmy," she said again. "Can you hear me?"

I nodded. Doing so made my heart hurt.

"Are you okay? How do you feel?"

"What're you doing here? Where am I?"

"We're in an ambulance," she said. "You were knocked unconscious."

I was in a gurney in the bright white back of an ambulance. She was sitting next to me, her head hovering over me.

It didn't feel like we were moving. I leaned up and looked around. The back doors were open. We were parked on the curb just a little way down from Union Bus Station. The street was filled with squad cars, their flashing lights refracting off the broken glass of the Blue Line Cafe windows that had rained down on the sidewalk moments before.

Everything began to spin and I grew lightheaded, but I closed my eyes and forced myself to keep my head up.

"You okay?" she asked, placing one hand on my forehead and the other on my hand. "What is it? You feel damp and clammy. Are you dizzy?"

"I'm okay. Just need a second."

Her touch felt familiar yet strained and foreign, even forced, almost comforting but too awkward to truly be.

I tried to remember how long it had been since she'd touched me like this. It was so long ago I couldn't recall. Beyond quick embraces of greeting and salutation over the years, the only thing I could come up with was the brief touch of a backhand on a fevered brow from early adolescence.

"What are you mixed up in, son?" she asked. "People are dead."

"Where's Clip?" I asked. "Is he—"

"Who? The young negro with you? He's talking to your father."

"He's not my fa—" I started, but caught myself.

At the mention of Collins, she glanced out into the night quickly, nervously. He was jealous over her attention and affection, guarded it aggressively. At least he did when I was a kid.

"I need to talk to him. What happened?"

"Evidently there was a shoot-out."

She pulled her hands back. Slowly, almost surreptitiously. First one then the other.

"No, to me. What happened to me?"

"In all the commotion something got turned over and hit your head and then your head hit the floor. The booth or a table or something. Hit you just right. You have bumps on the front and back of your noggin."

I felt for them. They were there all right. And big.

"Have you talked with your brother lately?" she asked.

I shook my head. "I've been wrapped up in some stuff for a while now. Haven't talked to much of anybody."

"I knew you hadn't spoken to me much, but I was hoping you had kept in touch—"

"He and I never talk much," I said. "Even less lately."

"I wish you would. For me."

"How are you?" I asked.

"I'm fine," she said. "Just fine."

Collins wouldn't allow her to be anything else. She only felt and thought and said what he permitted.

Sometimes I was filled with such anger toward her I could taste it like bile rising up into my mouth, but mostly I felt sorry for her.

She was weak. Always had been. It just wasn't really revealed until my dad died. She couldn't be alone, couldn't be without a man. She had to have someone to tell her what to do, to provide for her the illusion of control and safety. And Commander Collins was a man made for the job.

What little there was of her by then began fading away from the day he came into her life. There wasn't much. It didn't take long.

I lost both parents the day my dad died. And gained a tyrant—a bullying, rigid, always-right dictator—and the shell of something resembling my mom, which he pulled the strings of.

Perhaps that was too harsh. Perhaps that was the boy talking who was abandoned by his dad and then his mom.

Either way, I could forgive her her weakness. I could extend
understanding to a scared, vulnerable, widowed mother
with two boys. I could see her actions in a light tinged with
compassion, couldn't I? Surely I could do that for my own
mother. Lauren was convinced I could and I wanted her to
be right.

"You know you can talk to me," I said. "About
anything. I can help. If you ever want to—"

"Thank you," she said. "I know I can. Always been
such a sweet boy. That's why I don't understand all this
criminal business you're mixed up in."

I started to say something, to try to explain, but
decided against it. Instead, I sat up the rest of the way.

Head spinning, stomach lurching, I clutched the rail
of the gurney, feeling like I was going to pass out or throw
up or both.

"Honey, don't get up," Mom said. "Lie back down."

She started to touch me, then glanced quickly
through the open doors, and stopped when she saw Clip
and Collins walking up.

"Finish your little nap, sweetheart?" Collins asked.

"Darryl," Mom said.

It was the most I'd ever heard her say to him and I
thought it perhaps a small sign of hope.

The dizziness passed and I slowly eased off the
gurney and climbed down out of the ambulance. I turned
to give Mom a hand, but saw that she was already out,
standing beside Collins.

"Connie, would you excuse us?" Collins said. "I need
to talk to James officially."

She nodded. "But he needs to go to a hospital."

"You go on back home now," he said. "I'll be there

when I can. Don't wait up for me. Go on to sleep."

"Okay," she said softly. "Love you."

"You too."

She seemed to want to hug or kiss him, and maybe even made a slight move to, but stopped.

She turned to me, started to move toward me, glanced back at Collins and stopped.

"We need to get started," he said.

She nodded.

"Bye baby," she said to me with a small wave.

"Bye, Mom. Thanks for coming to check on me. I love you."

Something danced across her face, but she didn't say anything, just turned and walked away.

I looked at Clip. "What happened?"

"Somebody shot the shit out of the joint."

"Vanessa?"

He shook his head. "Got her, her big-headed bodyguard, and one of the waitresses."

"Me?" I asked, rubbing my head.

"Sorry 'bout that. I pulled the booth down on top of you."

"Don't mind me, fellas," Collins said. "I'm just the chief of police. I don't mind waiting."

"You see the shooters?"

He shook his head.

"James, just what the hell is going on?" Collins asked. "This is the second crime scene you've been at tonight. I've got a dead cop and three dead civilians." It was the first time I had ever heard him say so much as *hell*.

"That's what we're trying to find out."

"Maybe, but you know a lot more than you're saying,

pal. No way you got here so fast without knowing where you were going when I spoke to you in the parking lot of the Panther."

"I swear we didn't. We found out that she might be staying at the Cactus. We went there. Night clerk sent us here."

"You should've called me," he said. "Out of respect for Dana if not for me."

"Didn't even know she would be here. Everything happened so fast."

"I'm not sure I believe you, James," he said. "I don't think that's ever been the case before."

"When I mentioned her name, why didn't you tell me you had had her in custody?"

"Who?

"Vanessa Patrick," I said. "The victim in there. The woman Dana was supposed to be meeting at the Panther."

"You saying she's been in my jail?"

I nodded.

"I don't think she has. Hold on. I'll check."

"While you do that I need to borrow a phone," I said. "Need to check in with my captain."

"You're not a cop anymore," he said. "So you don't have a captain."

Chapter 22

"Jimmy?" Folsom said.

"Yeah?"

"You okay?"

"Yeah. Why?"

"You don't sound so good, son," he said. "And I haven't heard from you in a while."

I was in a phone booth on the corner across the street from the Blue Line Cafe. There were still several cops milling around, a few actually processing the crime scene.

"Yeah," I said. "Sorry. A lot has happened."

"But you're okay?"

"A little dizzy from a bump on the head. Weak. Exhausted. But I'm okay."

"Good," he said. "That's good."

We were quiet a moment.

"Hey Jimmy, can you hold on a minute?"

"Sure."

While he was gone, I thought about how I was going to tell him about Dana. I was dreading it, and really had no idea how to do it.

Best to just say it, I thought. Don't wait. First thing.

Just give it to him straight.

"I thought I might have news for you, Jimmy," he said. "But I don't. Not yet. Seems De Grasse has slipped away. But that's only for the time being. I promise you that."

"I'm afraid I have some news," I said. "And it's bad."

"Okay."

"It's Dana Shelby," I said. "He was shot and killed."

The line went quiet a long moment. A low hum. Some static. The desultory sound of our breathing. Nothing else.

"How?" he asked eventually.

I told him.

When I finished he was silent again for a long while, then said, "He was a good cop. Good father. Good husband. A good man."

I nodded, realized he couldn't see me, then said, "Sure seemed so to me."

"So it was a setup?"

"Looks like it."

"Which means we got him killed."

I thought about it. It wasn't the first time. The first time I had thought about it I had come to a similar conclusion.

"I did," I said.

"No, son. It's not on you alone. I guarantee you that."

And even though I didn't buy it, it meant something that he said it. I thought about how different Captain Folsom was from Chief Collins, how grateful I was to have had Henry Folsom as a boss and a . . . whatever else he was—not friend exactly, but certainly more than a commanding officer.

"Two things," he said. "We find Lauren so his death wasn't in vain. Then we find those responsible and make them pay their debt in blood."

"What's our next move?" Clip asked.

We were standing back over near the ambulance again, waiting on Collins.

"I have absolutely no idea."

He nodded and seemed to think about it. "And how that different from any other time?"

I managed a smile.

He was right. That was the job. Stumbling around in the darkness, being lied to and misled by some while others attempted manipulation, intimidation, and bribery, all while not giving in, not giving up.

But if that was the job, then which direction should I stumble in next?

"Any ideas?" I asked. "Whatta you think we should do?"

Before he could answer, Collins reappeared and began walking toward us.

"'Pends on what he say."

I nodded.

"Well?" I asked.

"According to my jailer, she's still in custody," he said.

Chapter 23

Collins's jailer was a middle-aged man with a big belly that hung down over his belt and a balding head with a thin halo of fine blond hair around it. Above his thick, dirty-blond mustache, his glasses left deep red indentations on his small nose.

We were standing with him in front of the cell that, according to his logs, Vanessa Patrick was still in.

It was empty.

It was me, Clip, Collins, the jailer, whose name was Grady, and a young officer named Fellows. As far as I could tell, there didn't appear to be anything wrong with the young cop and I wondered what had kept him out of the war.

"Sergeant Grady, do you see Vanessa Patrick in there?" Collins asked, his voice rich with the savoring of the condescension in it.

He had brought me and Clip along, claiming I'd accuse him of corruption and cover-up if he didn't. He was right.

"No sir, Chief," he said.

The simple, spartan jail was neat, orderly,

immaculate. Not dim or dungeon-like in any way, the humane holding area was well lit, the fresh air tinged with citrusy smelling cleaning chemicals. It was what I would expect from Collins, which is why I found the missing inmate so incredulous.

"We wouldn't keep an inmate here that long anyway, would we?" Collins was asking.

"No sir."

"And we wouldn't keep a female here at all, would we?"

"No sir, not beyond the initial booking, no."

"So?"

Grady rubbed the bald dome of his head and let out a big sigh as he studied the cell some more.

"I have no idea. I'm sorry. I don't know why she was never processed out or . . . I just don't know."

"Well," Collins said, "don't you think we should find out?"

"Yes sir."

"Gather all the information you can find, bring all the documentation you have, and be in my office in ten minutes."

Which was how exactly nine and half minutes later we were sitting in Collins's office with a very sweaty Sergeant Grady, logs open on his lap.

"She was picked up for prostitution," he was saying.

"Who was the arresting officer?"

"I didn't do the booking, so I don't know for certain, but according to this it was Smith and Homan."

Collins shook his head.

"Who?" I asked.

"The two detectives you were talking to in the

Panther Room parking lot."

"Average Sam and Tall Roy?" I said.

"Detective Sam Smith and Detective Roy Homan," he corrected, emphasizing the *detectives* but good.

"They're the ones who rousted us at the phone booth earlier tonight," I said. "No telling what would've happened if Shelby hadn't stepped in. We see them again at the Panther Room—his crime scene—and they start in on us again. Now this."

"You can run some red lights, can't you, boy?" Collins said. "Slow down, would you? Apply the brakes a bit. You see conspiracy and corruption everywhere."

"No," I said, "you do. Everywhere but in your department."

"If I planned on covering up anything, you wouldn't be here, would you?" he said. Then turning to Grady, asked, "Who processed her in?"

He looked at his logs. "Kid that was just with us. Fellows."

"Get 'em all in here?"

Before he realized what he was doing and who he was doing it in front of, Grady looked at his watch.

"The time is irrelevant, Sergeant."

"No sir, I know. It wasn't that."

The clock on the wall behind Grady said that it was about twenty after twelve.

"I can be here, they can be here," Collins said. "But even if I wasn't here, I give an order I expect it to be followed."

"Oh, yes sir. I know."

The nervous sweat on Grady's face kept causing his glasses to slide down his nose, and he kept jamming them back up with his index finger, as if poking himself between the eyes.

"Immediately."

"Yes sir."

A large drop of sweat plunged off the end of his nose and onto his mustache. Using his thumb and forefinger, he rubbed both sides of his bristly whiskers down several times, beginning in the center above his top lip and pushing down firmly.

"No matter the time," Collins said. "No matter the order."

"Absolutely. Yes sir. I was trying to figure where they'd be, where I can find them. That was all."

"Get to it, Sergeant."

"Yes sir," he said, jumping up and spilling the logs out of his lap.

"Slow down," Collins said.

"Yes sir."

"Watch what you're doing."

"Yes sir."

He clumsily gathered his things and awkwardly stumbled out of the room.

Observing Collins's interaction with Grady made me think of the kind of parents that produced nervous, insecure kids, and I was glad again that he didn't get to me until most of my childhood was over, and that I had resisted his attempts at tearing me down and controlling me every step of the way.

"You two," I said, shaking my head when Sam and Roy

walked in, attempting to do it the same way Sam had when he had seen me and Clip in the Panther Room parking lot.

"Both men glared at me, but didn't say a word.

"What's this about, Chief?" Sam asked.

With Grady looking for Fellows, it was only me, Clip, Collins, Sam, and Roy in the room.

"We hurt your kid's feelings or something?" Roy asked.

"Gee, we're really sorry," Sam said.

"Look boys," Collins said. "I usually cut you a lot of slack 'cause you're good cops and I like the way you handle the hoods in this town, but this is serious and it could cost you plenty. Whatta you say you skip all the cuteness and get on the level, and fast, okay?"

"Sorry boss," Roy said.

"We're tired," Sam said. "And a little loopy."

"And we lost a brother tonight, you know?" Roy added.

"Why I'm giving you boys a break," Collins said. "Just don't want you to mistake me and build your gallows any higher than you have to."

"Nobody mistakes you, Chief," Sam said. "Nobody."

The difference between the way Collins treated these two versus Grady reminded me of the difference in the way he treated me and my brother growing up. He had his favorites, and he enjoyed making their existences cushy nearly as much as making those not favored suffer.

"So tell me about this arrest," Collins said, pointing to the log book on the front edge of his desk facing them.

They both stepped forward and looked at it, neither bending over to see it any better.

"Pross we pinched for solicitation," Sam said.

"Simple as they get," Roy said.

"Name sound familiar?" Collins asked.

They nodded.

"We've arrested her a few times," Roy said. "Why?"

"That the only reason?"

They both appeared to think about it real hard.

They nodded.

"Think so, Chief," Sam said. "Why? We missin' somethin'?"

"Remember earlier tonight at the Panther Room?" Collins said. "James told us who Dana was there to meet?"

Sam did his thinking-hard look again. "Valerie something-another, wasn't it?"

"What about the vics at the Blue Line a little while ago?"

"We didn't catch that one," he said.

"And you haven't heard the names?"

"No sir," he said. "We just heard it wasn't your one-armed son and we were so relieved."

"You take chances, Sam," Collins said. "You really do."

"We been busy working Dana's case," Roy said.

"Oh yeah? Whatcha got so far for all of that?"

"Not much, Chief. Just gettin' started good."

"I see," Collins said. "Well, the woman Dana was supposed to meet and one of the victims from the Blue Line is none other than your pinched pross Vanessa Patrick."

"Really?" Roy said.

"Seriously?" Sam said.

"And according to that log right there she's still in my jail."

"You don't say," Roy said.

"I do," Collins said.

"You're kidding," Sam said.

"I don't," Collins said.

"So she got Dana killed?" Sam said. "Any idea who killed her?"

"So that's the way you're gonna play it, fellas?" Collins said. "I wouldn't if I were you."

"We're not playing anything, Chief," Sam said. "On the level. We're just as confused as you."

"I look confused?" Collins said.

What he looked was immaculate, his uniform crisp and tight and wrinkle free, his eyes clear and bright, his posture erect, no sign of whiskers on his face and not a single hair out of place. It was as if he had just arrived for work after a good night's sleep instead of the middle of the night after a long day with no sleep.

"No sir. I just meant . . . We don't know anything other than what we've told you."

"And if you really thought we did," Roy added, "do you think it's best to do this in front of a civilian and a nigger?"

"You're right," Collins said. "Don't know what I was thinking. I should have each of you in separate interview rooms."

Chapter 24

Collins went at both his men hard and for a while, and I wondered if it was for me, but figured it was far more likely that he actually believed they were lying and the idea of his being out of control of his own men, his own jail, his own world in any way, was intolerable.

I think that was what bothered him so much about me. He had been unable to control his own stepson, to break me, to mold me into his image and, therefore, I was intolerable for him.

Clip and I were in a dark observation room with a couple of one-way mirrors in it, watching through the translucent glass into the interview rooms.

Sam was sitting alone in his, stewing, waiting, while Collins was in Roy's room going at him.

We had front row seats to a police interrogation of police, something we shouldn't have had—something we wouldn't have had if Collins wasn't an authority unto himself. I hoped for his sake that Average Sam and Tall Roy were guilty or that internal affairs didn't find out about what he was doing.

"Don't look like they breakin'," Clip said.

Neither man had yet to say anything revealing or even suspicious, and unlike earlier they had dropped the caviler attitude and even the hint of insolence.

"No it doesn't."

"What we do if they don't?"

"Maybe they were acting the way they were because they truly had nothing to hide," I said.

"So what next?" he asked. "What we do if we get nothin' from them?"

"I have no idea," I said. "I'm at a loss again and all I can think of is Lauren's life is on the line and I don't know what to do, don't know how to save her."

"Gots to let that part go," he said. "Or collapse under the pressure of it."

I nodded slowly and frowned. "I know," I said, "but knowing that and being able to do that are two different things."

"I've told you everything, Chief," Roy was saying. "I'm on the level. Honest I am."

His voice came from within the interview room through a small speaker, low and a little garbled, not easy to understand.

"Can't tell you anything else 'less I start making it up," he said. "I've already told you everything I know. I swear it. I'm not hiding anything. Come on, Chief, you know me. I'm a good cop. Sam is too. You know we wouldn't be mixed up in somethin' criminal."

"If you're lying to me . . ." Collins said.

"I'm not. I swear on my life."

"If the way you played it in my office caused us to waste time and costs the girl her life . . ."

"What girl?" Roy said. "I thought she was dead."

"I know y'all can hear me," Sam said.

He was speaking loudly and looking toward us through the window.

"I know y'all are watching," he said. "Look soldier, I don't know everything that's going on, but whatever it is, my partner and I have nothing to do with it. I swear on my mother's life. You're wasting time on us when you could be trying to find out who really freed the hooker and killed our friend. Two things I'd be glad to help you with. Up to you, but if another cop gets killed or someone you care about, just remember I told you not to waste time on us."

"I think they're clean," Collins was saying.

He was back in the observation room with us.

"I know you'll think I'm covering up some kind of crime my department committed but—"

"I agree," I said.

"You do?"

I nodded.

"So cut 'em loose?"

"Yeah."

He nodded appreciatively. "They're cocky and full of themselves, but they're good cops."

"Grady track down who was working the desk the night Vanessa was taken out to play army nurse at Johnston's?"

"Must not have. He's bringing him here when he does. I'm gonna go let my guys go then we'll look for him."

I nodded.

When he left the room, I yawned and stretched. Clip

yawned in response and laughed.

"Don't care how tired you are," he said, "we ain't stopping 'til we find her."

I smiled. "Thanks for that," I said. "I was just about to give up."

"I hope you boys understand," Collins was saying, "I had to do it. And don't think I did it for anyone but me. I had to know for sure so we could move forward."

He had Sam and Roy in the same room. All three men were standing.

"You fellas are good cops," he said. "Now that Dana's gone, the best I got. I gotta be able to trust you, but good. I had to know."

They nodded.

"We understand, Chief," Roy said.

"Now," Collins said. "Go home. Get a little sleep. Get showered. Get back here in the morning ready to go."

"It one thing to think they not involved," Clip said. "It another to send they asses home for some sleep."

After a quick light tap on the door, Grady entered the observation room.

"Where's the chief?" he said.

I nodded toward the interview room, but the three men had already vacated it, and a moment later Collins was walking in.

"Whatta you got for me, Sergeant?" he said.

"Well, I confirmed with Fellows that it was Smith and Homan that brought in the Patrick dame," he said.

"Okay," he said. "But we knew that. They never said they didn't. We need to know who took her out."

"Fritz was working the night you asked me to check on," he said. "Says Smith and Homan were around, but he didn't see them take her out."

"Then who?"

"Don't you remember?" Grady said. "That was the night of the big fight."

"It was, wasn't it?" Collins said. "Big inmate brawl. Nobody seriously hurt, but took a while to break it up, then we had medics come in."

"That was to distract everyone while they snuck her out," I said.

"Who?" Grady said.

I shrugged. "Smith and Homan?"

He shook his head. "I was called in. Saw the aftermath firsthand. They helped break up the fight, helped separate them in different cells—oh hell."

"What?" Collins said. "And language, Sergeant."

"Hers was one of the cells we used to separate them. It was already empty by then."

"Because she was taken out during the fight," I said.

"Any of the inmates involved in the fight still in custody?" I asked.

Grady nodded.

"We need to talk to them. See who bribed them to fight."

Another knock on the door was followed by a sleepy-looking sergeant with thick black hair and a five o'clock shadow sticking his head in the door.

"We got an emergency call for Jimmy Riley," he said. "Panama City PD."

Collins nodded.

I followed the sergeant to a phone.

It was at an empty desk in the dim, vacant squad room.

"Riley," I said.

"Jimmy, it's Iris."

Iris was Henry Folsom's secretary. She had been for as long as I could remember. A kind but tough older lady who had acted more and more like a mother to Folsom as Gladys got worse and worse over the years, Iris was efficient and sensitive, and had always been particularly fond of me.

"It's Henry," she said.

It was the first time she had referred to him as anything but Captain Folsom.

"Yeah?"

"He's been shot. He's in the hospital. They're pretty sure De Grasse did it. He got away, but one of the witnesses said he had a woman with him matching Lauren's description."

Chapter 25

Henry Folsom's room had that middle-of-the-night quietness and dimness that was different in tone and quality from any other time.

He wasn't conscious, and I didn't know if he was sleeping or in a coma.

He was tall and large, with a big frame and a certain muscular thickness that he had managed to retain even past middle age, and he eclipsed the hospital bed beneath him.

On the drive back over from Tallahassee I had done what I had been doing all night—questioned whether I was doing the right thing. Was it right to return to Panama City? Was Lauren really here? Did Flaxon De Grasse have her? Was he preparing even now to make her his last work of art, his masterpiece?

Images of his victims had flashed in my mind. Horrific. Disturbing. Vivid. Continual.

All of them the same.

A beautiful woman in life . . . retaining a certain bloom in death.

No blood.

Skin impossibly white.

Hair impossibly dark.

Posed on black satin.

The high contrast between the background and her body was severe and served to heighten the shocking impact of the image, and though the photograph was black and white, the subject matter was such that it would've looked the same at the scene.

Her legs were spread open, her feet extended up and out. There was something subtly but decidedly sexual about the pose. Above her legs, the top half of her bloodless bisected body was only a few inches away, but had not been lined up precisely, so the two parts were slightly askew.

Her arms were up, one draped over her eyes, as if sleeping while shading from a bright light, the other bent so that her hand fell gently between her breasts.

But what if De Grasse didn't have Lauren?

Should I have stayed in Tallahassee? Should I be talking to inmates with Collins to see who staged the distraction in order to break Vanessa Patrick out?

The threat from De Grasse, if there was one, seemed more imminent than anything else, so I had made my decision, but that didn't mean I didn't doubt it, didn't mean I wouldn't drive myself crazy questioning whether what I was doing was ensuring I would lose Lauren forever. Or maybe I already had. Maybe every move I made was futile. There was no way to know and it had never mattered more.

I wasn't sure what to do, but I knew I had to stop in and see Henry before I did anything else.

Gladys couldn't be here. He was alone.

He had been more like a father to me than anyone since mine died, far more than Darryl Collins or even my old partner and father figure Ray Parker.

I couldn't not stop in for a moment to show concern, express respects, acknowledge all he had done for me.

I thought about how many times he and Gladys had me over for dinner, how often he'd call me to his office and hand me a brown paper bag lunch and say, "Gladys said you're looking a little too thin."

When my arm had been blown off, when my world had imploded in on me, when I lost Lauren and was as alone as I had ever been, it had been Henry and Gladys I had opened my eyes to in my lonely hospital room, Henry and Gladys who had visited every day, Henry and Gladys who had stayed until made to leave by the nurses.

I needed to find out where Gladys was and go see her. Should have already.

A nurse came in to check Folsom's vitals and startled when she saw me.

"Sorry," I said.

"What're you doing here? It's one-thirty in the morning. Visiting hours are long since—"

"I just got back in town," I said. "I had to see him for a second. I was about to go. Can you just tell me how he is."

"I'm afraid he's not good," she said. "He was shot. The bullet did a lot of damage. He survived surgery, but a man his age . . ."

"I ain't dead yet," he said.

We both turned toward him. I couldn't help but smile.

"Well hey, Captain Folsom," she said. "Welcome back."

"So you can't start planning my funeral just yet," he said.

"I was just telling your son that a man as big and strong and mean as you eats bullets for breakfast and will be just fine. Just fine."

"Lady, lying to a cop is not a smart thing to do. Now, excuse me and this young man for a couple of minutes. We got important police business."

"I don't know . . ."

"Yes you do. Grant a dying man his wish. Come back in a few minutes. If I'm still kicking you can kick him out. Hell, he looks worse than I do. Look at the size of that knot on his head."

Finally, begrudgingly, she left.

"What happened to your head?" he asked.

"I bumped it."

"And your gut . . . did you reopen the wound? You're bleeding."

"Skip it," I said. "I'm fine. How are you? Really."

"Doesn't matter," he said. "Listen. I'll be fine. Or I won't. But you've got to find Lauren. I think De Grasse has her."

Flaxon De Grasse had pretended to be a surrealist art gallery owner named Adrian Fromerson. He was a dainty, diminutive man, gaudy and gaunt. He had bleach-blond hair that was short and stood up in jagged clumps, and his skin was pasty. He looked nothing like what he was—a vicious, brutal butcher the likes of which I had never heard of.

"And if anything does happen to me," he was saying, "I need you to look after Gladys."

"I hope you know you don't have to ask."

"I know how you feel about Lauren," he said. "You'd do anything for her, wouldn't you?"

I nodded.

"Anything?"

"Anything," I said.

"Well, imagine how much more true it'd be if you'd been together over thirty years."

I nodded again. I understood what he was saying, though I couldn't imagine being any more in love, any more willing to do anything for Lauren than I was now.

"If you make it out of this and I don't," he said, "take care of my girl."

"I will."

"If I make it out of this and you don't, I'll take care of yours," he said. "Swear it."

I nodded. "I know," I said. "So tell me what happened."

"I played a hunch," he said. "Knew the net we had around him was tight. Knew he had very few options. Couldn't get out of town. Couldn't hide very many places. So I figured he might go back to someplace familiar, someplace we wouldn't suspect because he'd been there before. I didn't have any men to spare, so I went myself."

"Where?"

"The old house," he said. "Victorian in St. Andrews with the art where he left his last victim before he disappeared."

As Adrian Fromerson, De Grasse had owned and operated a kind of surrealist art gallery in an old three-story Victorian house in St. Andrews and actually assisted in the investigation.

"I searched the place," he was saying. "Thought it

was clean. Was actually walking back downstairs to leave. He turned the corner to come up the stairs. Don't think he knew I was there. We both drew. He fired first. Three shots. One got me. I hesitated because . . . he had a . . . someone with him. I think it was Lauren."

"Any idea where he went?"

He shook his head slowly.

"I went down. All I could do was try not to tumble down the stairs. I'm sorry. I should've . . . He left. Eventually, I made it down and called for help. Neighbor heard him screeching away and looked out. Gave a description of him and a girl that looked like Lauren."

"Times up, soldier."

I turned to see the nurse coming into the room.

I didn't move.

"I mean it," she said. "I can have a cop thrown out of here just like anybody else. Soldier too."

"Just one more—"

"No," she said. "I already let you stay longer than I should have. Out. Now."

I stood.

"Thank you for all you've done for me," I said. "All of it. Get better. Don't worry about a thing. I'll find Lauren. You'll get better. We'll both be around to take care of our girls."

"But . . . if either of us isn't . . ." he said.

I nodded. "Count on it," I said, and walked out.

Chapter 26

On my way out, I saw Iris sleeping in the waiting room. Slumping in an uncomfortable chair, head back, mouth open slightly. Snoring.

She was the only one in the small waiting room.

"Iris," I said softly.

I stayed a few feet away, not wanting to hover over her as she opened her eyes.

"Iris."

She slowly blinked her eyes open, lifted her head, and wiped her mouth.

"Jimmy," she said, and seemed genuinely happy to see me. "You came."

"Of course."

"Have you been in to see him?"

I nodded. "Just walked out."

"What happened to your head?" she said, alarm in her voice. "And you're bleeding through your shirt. Are you all right?"

"I'm fine," I said.

"You sure?"

I nodded.

She slowly stood and stretched.

"How is he?"

"He's okay," I said. "Weak, but otherwise seemed . . ."

"He needs to slow down," she said. "Just be a captain, not feel like he's got to be on the frontline, you know?"

I nodded.

We were quiet a moment.

No one else in the entire hospital was visible—not a single soul down either corridor—and it was as if we were the only two people in an abandoned building in the middle of the night.

"What are you doing here?" I asked.

She shrugged. "Who else is gonna be? Poor Gladys is in very bad shape. Did you know she's in a sanatorium? None of the detectives will come—except maybe to see him once, later, if he survives. He has no one."

"Except you."

"I ain't much, fella, but I'm present and accounted for."

I smiled.

"Where is Gladys?" I asked.

"I told you. A sanatorium."

"Which?"

"Oh," she said. "Sorry. I'm a little out of it. She's in a real nice place called Oak Cove."

"I need to go see her as soon as I can."

"Go tonight if you can."

I must have looked surprised.

"No, really," she said. "She doesn't sleep. I usually go late at night. Staff prefers it. Just don't tell her he got shot. It'll upset her and then a little while later she wouldn't even remember you said it."

I nodded. "Probably won't be tonight, but I will soon."

"Killed him to have to put her in there. He's such a fine man," she said, nodding in the direction of Folsom's room. "All he's done for that woman. All he went through to try to keep her at home. All he went through to get her the best place possible. And still he's wracked with guilt."

I nodded and we were quiet another quick moment.

"Who's heading up the search for De Grasse now?" I asked.

She shook her head and frowned. "You're not gonna like it."

"Butch?"

She nodded. "Butch."

I let out a long, frustrated sigh.

"No choice," she said. "With no replacement for Pete yet, we're undermanned and Butch is ranking."

"It's rank all right," I said. "You called that one. And good."

I had dropped Clip by his place before going to see Henry Folsom so he could bathe and change before we started looking for De Grasse, and I decided to swing by the office to pick up some fresh clothes and ammo of my own before picking him up again.

Harrison was hopping—had been all night every night since the start of the war. I had to park an entire block down from my office and dodge people on the sidewalk to get to it.

As I neared the door to the walkup that used to be the Parker Detective Agency, a car door opened and a short, young Asian man stepped out and ushered me in.

I recognized the car.

It was a six-passenger Presidential Delux-style Land Cruiser with a black roof, whitewall tires, and a back glass with ventilating wings. It belonged to Miki Matsumoto's uncle, a Japanese-American fugitive from an internment camp in California.

He was a thick, middle-aged man with thick black hair and thick orangish skin. Like the first time I had met him, he was wearing a three-button tan Glen Plaid sports coat and solid medium brown wool slacks with pleats and cuffs, a hand-painted tie in a thick Windsor knot, and brown and tan wingtips.

"Miki is ah missing again," he said without greeting or preamble. "You find."

Miki Matsumoto was a Japanese teen who had been abducted on Panama City Beach. I had found her and returned her to her mother and uncle just a few days ago. She had been beaten and raped repeatedly and was no doubt traumatized.

"How long?"

"Two day."

"Any idea where she might be?"

He shook his head.

From an unseen source, Tommy Dorsey's "In the Blue of the Evening" was playing, and as usual, the man known as the sentimental gentleman of swing was proving just how smooth-toned a trombone could be.

"Where was she when she went missing?" I asked. "Who was she with?"

"You ah talka to ah mother and friend tomorrow," he said. "I ah pick youa upa in back tomorrow noon."

"I'm working a case right now," I said. "I'll be here if I can."

"You be here or we kill one-leg girl."

I had pushed Ruth Ann and her brutal slaying from my mind until this moment.

"Somebody beat you to it, pal," I said.

"Then you or ah somebody else you care about."

As much as I felt bad for Miki Matsumoto, as much as I wondered what had happened to her and wanted to help find her again, I had no intention of doing anything until I found Lauren. But it did me no good to let him know that, so I just nodded.

"You ah very ah persuasive," I said. "See you ah in back of ah here tomorrow noon."

I walked up the stairs to my office wondering what could've happened to the kid. Her uncle and his men had killed the man responsible for her abduction, imprisonment, torture, and rape after burning his place to the ground, so I knew it wasn't him. Did he have a partner? Had I missed something?

I was so deep in thought, so exhausted, so out of it, I didn't realize someone was in my office until some sixty seconds after I should have.

I reached under my coat for my gun as I approached the top of the stairs, but didn't withdraw it once I saw who it was.

Sitting there behind what once was July's reception

desk, lit only by the pale glow of the desk lamp, was the young Japanese girl I was supposed to be looking for. Miki Matsumoto.

I blinked several times to make sure it was really her.

She smiled up at me, her bruised face small and beautiful, wincing as she stood and made her way over to me.

"Miki? What're you doing here?"

"I work for you now," she said.

She removed my hat and started taking off my coat.

In my confusion I let her before I realized what I was doing.

I shook my head, wincing at the pain that caused. "You don't work for me," I said. "You don't owe me anything."

She reached up with her tiny hand and touched the bump on my forehead. Her fingers were cold, her touch tender and felt good on the swollen spot, and I realized how cold the office was.

"Thank you," I said.

She gave a slight bow.

"I be very good worker for you," she said. "Help you help other poor soul like me."

"Your uncle is looking for you," I said. "He was just outside."

Her eyes grew wide in alarm and she looked over my shoulder toward the staircase.

"He's gone," I said. "But he'll be back. You have to go home."

She shook her head. "I am disgrace. Defiled now. No man want me but old, dirty man. They make me marry him. Say it only thing for me to do. I not go back. I work for you. I already work for you. Clean office."

I looked around. The office was as clean as I had ever seen it.

"I not just wait for you. Work. I be very much good for you. But we talk later. You have man here to see you. Wait very long time. He in here."

She turned and led me to Ray's office.

Who would be here in the middle of the night? Surely she's confused.

"This your office?" she asked.

I shook my head. "That one," I said, indicating mine. "But it's okay. This is fine."

"Sorry. Get right next time, boss," she said, then gave a small bow and walked back over to July's desk.

When I opened the door, I was surprised at who I saw standing there, but I shouldn't have been.

"Burke," I said.

"Soldier."

Coleman Burke, a small, thin man with a boyish face, was the best hired gun this side of Miami—maybe the other side too. Emotionless, exacting, precise, professional.

"What can I do for you?" I asked, closing the door behind me.

"I was hired to kill you," he said.

"Then I'm dead," I said.

He nodded.

The last time I had seen him he had just shot a woman in the center of her forehead. He had been hired to kill me then too, only the guy who hired him was killed before he had a chance to do it so the job expired instead of me.

I tried to figure any angle I could, any way to stay

alive for Lauren, but it was no good. If I went for my gun, he'd put a hole in me before the tips of my fingers even grazed it.

I couldn't have drawn faster than him even when I had my right arm. With only my left it was even less than hopeless.

What would happen to Lauren? Would Clip and Henry Folsom find her? Would Clip try to square this with Burke and get killed himself and not be able to help Folsom, Lauren, or anyone else?

"Who?" I asked.

"Come on, soldier, you know I can't tell you that."

I nodded.

Unlike everyone else I had encountered since it happened, he hadn't asked about the bump on my head or the blood on my shirt. He didn't care. They were irrelevant to his mission—except to make it easier.

"Who was I working for the last time I saw you?" he said. "Oh that's right. Mickey Adams. What was the fat bastard's name that—"

"Truman Jackson Weller," I said.

"That much fat, you kind of need three names, don't you?" he said.

I smiled.

"You cleaned up all that real good," he said. "Saved me a lot of hassle—or worse."

I nodded. "That worth anything to you?"

"What? Like your life?"

"Maybe not that much," I said. "But something."

He thought about it then nodded. "Why I'm here," he said. "Figure I owe you something."

"Such as?"

He shrugged. "Not sure."

If I thought it would help I'd tell him about Lauren and what I was trying to do, but it was irrelevant to him and what he did. It had to be. It didn't matter that I was one of the good guys or that whoever hired him wasn't. Nearly all of the people who hired him were wicked, and nearly all of the people he was hired to kill didn't deserve it. It didn't matter. He was hired to do a job and he did it. He was good at it in part because the whos and whys didn't enter into it for him.

"I'd offer you a running start," he said, "but I know you wouldn't take it."

The reason Burke was here, the reason I was able to do what I did, was because of the code I lived by—a code not as dissimilar from Burke's as you might imagine. My word was good. If I said I'd do something, I did it. My morality was not completely contingent on legality. I would never shoot anyone in the back. I came at you straight. Dealt with you like a man—even if you were a criminal. I could never be bought off. Scared off. Once hired, I worked a case 'til it was done. No matter what. Burke knew these things about me, knew I could be trusted. And over the years I had done a good turn or two for him. All of which might be about to save my life and, in the process, Lauren's.

"Not under normal circumstances," I said.

"You wouldn't run under any circumstances," he said.

I tilted my head and shrugged. "Actually . . ."

"Spill," he said. "See if you can make me believe it."

I did.

He thought about it for a long time.

"You're a stand-up guy, soldier," he said. "You don't run. You don't scare. You . . . You'd let a dame make you run?"

"If it meant I could save her."

He looked genuinely perplexed. What I was saying just didn't track for him.

"You're not a coward," he said.

"No," I said, "I'm not."

"You don't back down. You don't walk away. You damn sure don't run."

"For her," I said, "I would."

He shook his head.

Not for the first time I had the thought that I might not be made out of the right metal for this work. Maybe what Collins told Dana Shelby was right. Maybe I'm not cut out to be a cop or detective or soldier or tough guy of any kind, and maybe I wasn't even before I lost my arm or fell in love with Lauren Lewis.

"Then run," he said. "I'll give you a day. Then I'm coming for you."

Chapter 27

"Anything happens to me, you'll still find Lauren and take care of her, won't you?" I said.

Clip looked over at me from the passenger seat, studying me a long moment before saying anything.

I had gotten Miki Matsumoto my old room at the Cove Hotel, had picked up Clip, and we were now headed toward St. Andrews.

I had been concerned that Miki might be uncomfortable staying there by herself or too fearful given the hell she had just experienced in a hotel room, but I needn't have been. She was sound asleep before I made it to the door.

"Why you think you gots to ask?"

"I just wouldn't want you thinking you had to square something for me. Lauren is all that matters."

"Where this comin' from?" he asked.

I shrugged and shook my head. "I know it goes without saying, but I felt the need to say it."

"Oh, you just felt the need to say it all of a sudden," he said. "Out of the blue?"

I nodded.

We were driving down Eleventh Street in a night that had grown gradually darker and colder, our half headlamps no match for the low fog hovering over the road. The street was empty and there didn't seem to be any movement anywhere around us for miles.

Four or five hours 'til dawn. Would the rising sun, when it arrives, bring hope or only a less dim despair? Would I even be here to see it?

He said, "Didn't have nothin' to do with going to your office? Your two previous partners being dead? The place haunted for you? You run into they ghost?"

"Somethin' happens to me," I said, "means somebody made it happen. All I'm sayin', I want you to let it go. Just find Lauren and bring her home. Make sure she's okay."

"Who threaten you?" he asked.

"You think I'm cut out for this kind of work?" I asked.

"Jesus, Jimmy. What the hell happen while I was bathin' my black ass?"

"I want an honest answer," I said.

"Only kinds I gots. You wants to know whether you's cut out for thuggery or not?"

"For what I do, for what we do . . . for what we've been doin' together for the past few years."

"You think I be runnin' these streets with you if I didn't think you was?"

"That's not a real answer."

"Hell it ain't," he said.

"Okay," I said, deciding to let it go.

"You different," he said. "That what you want me to say? Told you that earlier when you's busy tellin' me I didn't owe you nothin' for what you did for me."

I thought back to our earlier conversation. It seemed like several days instead of some nine hours ago.

"I ain't your friend 'cause of what you did for me," he said. "And I don't help you 'cause I feel like I owe you. But I ain't sayin' what you did got nothin' to do with 'em."

I nodded.

"World need a man like you," he said. "So do detecting and thuggery. Way you do it—your fuckin' code and conscience and all—may make it harder, may even mean you don't do it as long. Don't mean you ain't meant for it. Hell, it may even mean you's made for it."

At first I couldn't say anything. He'd never said anything like that to me before—no one had—and I was touched beyond telling.

The intervening silence was neither awkward nor pregnant, and he sat there comfortably, feeling no need to say anything else.

Eventually I managed a "Thank you," and that was the end of it.

We searched Adrian Fromerson's art gallery and anarchists meeting house thoroughly, guns drawn.

The huge house was more meeting hall and museum than home, with books and brochures in the foyer, a lecture hall in the living room, crooks and crannies of couches and pillows and a surrealist art installation everywhere else.

From the outside, it appeared to be an old three-story Victorian, but inside it was both bohemian and radical.

Clip and I moved methodically through the creaky hardwood-floored house searching every possible space De Grasse could be hiding in, the works on the walls around us disturbing and disquieting, combining distorted images, odd perspectives, eerie elements, asymmetrical arrangements.

Human bodies, mostly women, deconstructed, disassembled, rearranged. Elongated humans with the heads of animals. Female torsos cut open with manger scenes and city skylines inside them. Men with erect penises and boat oars for legs. Heads coming out of navels. Shapes. Impressions. More semblance of things than actual depictions of the things themselves.

I recalled Adrian Fromerson leading me through here the first time, remembered some of what he had said . . . "See how the work involves elements of surprise, non sequiturs, and unusual and unexpected juxtapositions? What you're seeing is liberation. A truth beyond the real, a kind of sur-real truth that transcends the obvious and actual."

I had been so close to him. How many lives could I have saved if I had known he was actually Flaxon De Grasse? Would Lauren be back with me now? Would Ruth Ann still be alive?

We continued to the second floor, passing Henry Folsom's blood on the staircase. The paintings and sculptures there were far better than those on the first, their juxtapositions more startling, their disjointedness and disorientation more disconcerting, more sexual and colorful and radical.

But nothing compared with the third floor where De Grasse had placed his own work, including, eventually, displaying one of his victims. It was a single room known as Black and White Butchery and looked nearly identical to the crime scene photos of De Grasse's female victims.

All black, including the floor. Faceless female mannequins painted white were posed on black silk drop cloths in various stages of disassemble and dissection, the poses identical to those De Grasse had used in arranging and displaying his victims.

"Be a fuckin' service to humanity to put this motherfucker down," Clip said.

I nodded. "Somethin' I should've already done."

"You hear they's bastards like this," he said, "but you don't believe it. Not really."

I thought again about what was done to Ruth Ann, how I had been made to watch, how the inhumanity and butchery didn't seem real even after witnessing it with my own eyes.

After completing our search of the entire house, which meant having to walk through Henry Folsom's blood twice, it was evident Flaxon De Grasse was long gone.

"What now?" Clip asked.

"The dock house," I said.

Flaxon De Grasse was supposed to have lived at the end of a dock in a small shack on St. Andrew's Bay. When we had investigated it earlier we found a rickety dock, the gaps in its planks like missing teeth in a demented smile, leaning pilings and empty slips, the entire structure appearing abandoned and soon to be at the bottom of the bay. There was no sign that De Grasse had ever lived there, and though there was a workshop with the tools necessary for what he was doing to the women he killed, there was no evidence he ever had used them or that location to do so.

"Thought that place's just a decoy?" Clip said.

"Doesn't mean he wouldn't use it to hide in now," I

said.

"True," he said.

I killed the lights of the old Victorian and opened the front door.

When we walked out Butch was standing there with a couple of uniform cops waiting on us.

Chapter 28

"Well well," Butch said. "Would you lookie here?"

"Butch," I said.

"Jesus, Jimmy, you don't look so good," he said. "I mean even worse than usual."

He was an overweight older man with a dark complexion, stubble, some scar tissue around his eyes, and a nose that had been broken more than once.

"You two are under arrest," he said.

I shook my head—even though it hurt to do so.

Butch was a bully and a bad cop. He had moved up from Miami or down from Chicago—I had heard both—a couple of months ago and partnered with my old partner on the force, Pete Mitchell. He was slow and mean and had been trying to put the pinch on me since the moment we met.

"Breaking and entering. Disturbing a crime scene."

"Not gonna let you arrest us tonight," I said.

"What?" he asked in genuine shock. "Ain't gonna let me? You ain't got a choice in the matter, pal."

"Captain Folsom sent us here," I said.

"Nice try pal, but Folsom's in the hospital."

"Which is where I saw him," I said. "Call him if you like. Or if you don't want to disturb him, and I wouldn't, I was you, then call Iris. I saw her too. She's in the waiting room."

He shook his head. "What're you playin' at, peeper?"

I didn't say anything.

"You take chances, dontcha?" he said. "One day you're gonna push it too far and I'm gonna bury you."

"Remember the woods, Butch?" Clip said.

Butch had taken me to the woods to torture and interrogate me—maybe even kill me. Clip and I got the jump on him and could have easily given him early retirement, something I was inclined to do when I thought he might have had something to do with what happened to Pete Mitchell and to Lauren. To his surprise we had let him go after he had convinced me he had nothing to do with either disappearance or death.

"You could be rotting in an unmarked grave right now," Clip continued. "We're the good guys."

Butch looked at me. "No nigger's gonna talk to me like that, understand? Final warning. And just 'cause you ain't got the rocks to kill a cop, don't mean you a good guy."

"Look, Butch, we think De Grasse has Lauren Lewis," I said. "All we care about is finding her. That's it. Hassle us all you want after that."

"Thought the Lewis dame was dead," he said.

"We're going now," I said.

"Where you think you're goin'?"

"I just told you. To find De Grasse."

"Entire department's lookin' for him, but a one-armed dick and a one-eyed nigger's gonna find him?"

We started walking away when another uniform ran up from the car.

"Sergeant. Sergeant," he yelled. "We got another. There's another."

"Another what?" Butch asked.

"Another body. Like the others. The surrealist sex killer has struck again."

My heart stopped beating and my knees buckled. As my legs began to give, Clip grabbed my arm and helped me stay up.

"Where?" I said. "Where is she?"

"Not far from here," he said. "A little shack at the end of an old dock on the bay."

Clip drove.

We got there before Butch.

One of my old friends from the force let us through.

We ran down the dock, trying to avoid the missing planks, but not being too careful. It was too dark to see well enough anyway.

Like before, all the windows and doors were open. Unlike before, there was movement inside. A few cops moving around nervously.

The cold breeze was damp and dank and smelled of rotting fish and something else—death. Beneath the dock, desultorily, the unseen waters of the bay slapped, tapped, and punched the pilings.

The leaning structure consisted of two rooms.

The living area was just as before—smallish wood room, wind coming through the boards, a cot, a small kitchen table with one chair, an old, scarred wardrobe, a rocking chair, and stacks of papers and books. Framed paintings leaned against the walls, none of it hung, all of it De Grasse's work, trash and wine bottles littering the floor.

Apart from the body and the blood, the workshop was much the same—dirty and disorganized, littered with trash and bottles, old and well-worn tools, chains and hooks dangling from the ceiling, clinking together in the wind, and protruding from the walls, all holding the dismembered parts of white mannequins.

And now the actual body parts of his latest victim.

The wet copper smell of blood, the foul, slightly sweet-tinged stench of bisected bowel, the acrid ammonia aroma of urine—the olfactory equivalent of death.

This was nothing like before. Before he had made art of bloodless bodies, arranging their cleaned and pristine parts into surreal displays. This was rushed. This was ugly. This wasn't creative or artistic. This was a big bloody mess. Why? I knew why he was rushed, but why do it at all while on the run, while being pursued relentlessly? What's he up to?

Clip rushed in before me.

"Hey. Hey. What're you doing?" a cop yelled.

"Just need to see her face. Her face. Where is it?"

"Who the hell are you?" one cop said, while another said, "Over there," and nodded toward a hook in the corner that held her head.

We both turned and looked.

Unable to stop myself, my momentum had carried me into the room right behind Clip. I was close enough to see the horror with my own eyes.

"Jimmy?" one of the other cops said.

The disembodied head was tear-streaked and blood-covered, its skin pale and waxy, but I could tell instantly it wasn't Lauren.

"Get them the fuck outta here," Butch barked as he rushed in behind us.

A couple of cops started toward us, but we held up our hands and walked out on our own without protest.

Walking back down the long dock, attempting to avoid the missing planks, I was weak-kneed and punch-drunk, completely and utterly spent, but relieved and strangely relaxed, as if my body no longer had the strength or capacity for even the slightest tension.

"Why take the time to do that?" Clip said.

I turned and looked back at the leaning shack—now crime scene—and the cops swarming around it.

Clip added, "Just can't help himself? Can't stop? Even when he tryin' to get away."

I shook my head. "He's driven all right and he enjoyed that and good," I said. "But look."

He turned and looked back down the dock with me, as more cops passed by us on their way to the shack.

"Hell," I said, "practically every cop on duty is down there."

"Diversion," Clip said.

I nodded.

"But the roadblocks still up," he said. "This ain't gonna change that."

I started to say something and then it hit me.

"Look," I said, directing his attention to the right, to the

marina a mile or so away and all the boats moored there.
"Not usin' a road," Clip said. "Son of a bitch."

Chapter 29

We jumped in the car and raced around toward the marina, hopeful and suddenly energized.

"We don't find him at this one," Clip said, "he might be at another—public or private."

I nodded. "He uses this one," I said, "he escapes sooner and spends far less time on the road—possibly being spotted or hittin' a roadblock."

He nodded.

We were quiet a moment.

I was driving. There was no traffic on the road and with all the cops at the crime scene, I drove just as fast as I wanted, as I could.

"You gonna tell me what that was about?" Clip asked.

"What what was about?"

"The 'would I still find Lauren and take care of her and not square anything that might happen to you' what," he said.

"Just what it was," I said. "Just making sure."

"Could be wrong," he said, "but I's pretty sure this the first thing you lied to me about."

"I'll explain after we find her," I said.

"And if you gets killed 'fore we do?"

"Then you'll know what I meant."

"What I figured," he said, nodding to himself.

We reached the marina, parked, and began looking around.

We checked each slip, each boat, working our way quickly but carefully down the first row.

At the end, partially hidden by a bait and tackle shack on one side and a covered slip on the other, was a parked patrol car.

"We involve him?" Clip asked.

"Don't see as we have any choice," I said.

He nodded and we walked over to the car, making sure not to look like crazed surrealist sex killers as we did.

When we got close and the cop didn't flash his lights or open the door to get out, I figured he was walking around, patrolling the place on foot.

When we got closer I found out what he was really doing.

The beat cop, a big bald man named Kieser, was slumped in the seat, head forward, throat slit, shirt blood-soaked, lap a crimson puddle.

"He's here," I said. "Let's split up and find him."

Clip nodded.

"Two rows left," I said. "You take the next one. I'll get the one after that."

Guns drawn, we split up and began going slip by slip, boat by boat, down the two remaining rows.

It took a little while, but I completed the search of my row, continually checking the bay for boats in case he had already shoved off as I did.

There was no sign of him. Maybe he'd left long before we got here. Maybe this was another decoy. Maybe Kieser getting his throat cut had nothing to do with De Grasse. Maybe I'd never find Lauren. Maybe I'd be dead soon anyway.

I looked around but found no sign of Clip, so decided to walk back over to his row and help him finish the search.

It didn't take long to find him.

He was in a boat in the third slip up from the bottom.

He was standing there staring at me.

It took me a minute to make out Flaxon De Grasse behind him, gun to his head, using him for a shield.

"Riley," he said when he saw me. "Should've known."

Clip looked at me and frowned. "Sorry," he said. "He got the jump on me 'fore I knowed what was happenin'. Fuckin' up a lot tonight."

I shook my head and waved off his apology.

De Grasse was immaculately dressed dandy. His bleach-blond hair was short and looked electrified. His skin was pasty, but only showed on his face and hands. Every other inch of him was covered in a blood-splattered black European suit, white shirt, and tie. He stood at just under five feet. Clip, not a large man himself, completely eclipsed him until he moved.

I continued edging closer until I was at the edge of the dock, nearly able to reach out and touch the boat.

"Where's Lauren?" I asked.

The fine features of his small, pale face fractured into an enormous smile and expression of pure delight as he let out a little gleeful squeal.

"Oh," he said. "This is too good. You think I have her."

The boat rocked back and forth gently, rhythmically, Clip and De Grasse mirroring its movements, which reflected those of the bay.

"I don't have her," Flaxon was saying. "Oh, I wanted her. I really did. The art I could've made out of her already artful perfection . . . But no. Alas, what will happen to her is far, far worse than anything I could do to you or her. With what I do the suffering is over so quickly. The art lasts, but the suffering doesn't. Oh, she is so going to suffer—and so are you now. I can't believe no one told you. Guess Harry was going to but you killed him before he could."

Looking at this little man made me wonder again how such a small and odd-looking boy-man could have done the things he had done, could be such a brutal butcherer of beauty and innocence.

"Are you ready?" he asked. "Don't you want me to tell you? Isn't the suspense killing you? You better sit down."

"Tell me where she is and we'll let you live," I said.

He laughed in genuine amusement.

"I'll tell you where she is before I kill you and the nigger," he said. "She's in hell. A lasting torment and torture concocted for her by a truly wicked man.

"She's been nursed back to health—well, as healthy as she can get—then treated like the whore she is. Drugged, but not so much that she doesn't know what's going on, bound, gagged, she is tied to a bed in a whore house, being used and abused and defiled and re-diseased by every fat, ugly fucker who pays to put his limp prick in one of her whore holes. Think about it. Right now your precious Lauren is being fucked by a stranger. Some hairy, sweaty—"

He stopped mid-sentence as a flap of his bleach-blond hair and scalp blew off and brain and blood started running down his face and neck and he collapsed onto the deck of the boat, dead where he lay.

Clip grabbed his own ear and jumped forward.

I turned toward the sound of the shot to see Coleman Burke standing down the dock a short distance, his gun already holstered again.

"What the hell are you doing?" I yelled.

"Only thing I ever do," he said. "What I was paid to."

Chapter 30

"Burke the reason you sayin' all that shit earlier?" Clip asked.

We were back in the car driving down Beck Avenue. I didn't respond.

"De Grasse not the only one he hired to take out, is he?"

I still didn't say anything.

"Speak up," he said. "I'm still havin' a hard time hearing. Head's all fucked up from almost getting blowed off and gettin' some crazy fucker's blood and brain splattered on it."

Beck was empty.

We were driving down it looking for a payphone. I was going to call to check in with Collins because I didn't know what else to do.

"Why didn't he take us out too?" Clip asked. "Been easy to do. Three shots instead of one. You, me, and that blond bastard?"

"He gave me a day head start," I said.

"To run?"

I nodded.

He was quiet a moment thinking about it.

We passed by the ornate, opulent, and lushly landscaped Oak Cove and I thought of Gladys all alone in her hospital bed—the way her husband of over thirty years was in a different room in a different building across town, and it made me sad. Life is loss, I thought. We lose everything eventually, everything in the end.

I should stop and see her, should check on her and hug her and let her know she's not alone, but I couldn't. I just didn't have the time right now. I couldn't do anything but search for Lauren.

Gladys alone in her bed made me wonder what kind of bed Lauren was in and if anyone was in it with her. Was De Grasse telling the truth? Was she being viciously and repeatedly violated right now?

"You act like he already took you out," Clip said.

"Huh?"

"Him punchin' your ticket inevitable?"

"He could've done it tonight," I said. "I'd've never known he was there. Never known what happened. Just be dead. Flame burning one second. Snuffed out the next. I'm no match for him."

"And you think I not either," he said. "That why you say don't try to square anything, just find Lauren and take care of her."

"Burke's the best," I said.

"Best what?"

"Shooter."

"So I challenge him to a chess match."

"Hear he's pretty good at that too."

He laughed. "How you get a day out of him?"

I told him.

"He know you a stand-up guy," he said. "You willing not to be for love confused the little fucker."

"Guess it did."

"You willing to . . . to not be you, to be somethin' you disrespect—hell, that you detest—for Lauren."

I nodded. "'Cept . . . guess that means it is me."

He seemed to need a moment to think about that one. I gave it to him.

"What that thing 'bout honor you say?"

Instinctively, nearly involuntarily, I let out a harsh, humorless laugh.

"The Lovelace line," I said. "'Yet this inconstancy is such as you too shall adore. I could not love thee, dear, so much loved I not honor more.'"

"What about that?"

I thought about it.

"'Thought you believed that," he said.

"I did too."

"You don't?"

I thought about it some more. "Guess I don't."

I was confronted with being a hypocrite, with being full of shit, with abandoning my code, and I tried to figure out why. Were there things I wouldn't do for Lauren, for love? There were. This just wasn't one of them.

"What do you believe in?"

"Lauren," I said. "Love. That love matters more than honor, that love is honorable, a higher honor."

"Actin' dishonorable for love is honorable?" he asked.

I thought about it.

"How?" he said.

"Huh?"

"How dishonorable you willing to be? How far you willing to fall?"

I shrugged. "Not sure. Sort of making this up as I go along."

He laughed. "You'll run," he said. "Will you back-shoot Burke?"

Before I could respond, before I could even think about what he was asking me, I had a sudden and jarring jolt. A flash of an image. I thought of love and honor. I thought of what we do for love. I thought of Lauren and what I was willing to do to find her. I thought of the gangster in his pajamas in his comfortable hotel room, Henry alone and lonely in his simple, serviceable hospital bed, Gladys alone and confused in hers in the nice nursing home. I thought of the dead and how they haunted us, the living—if we are living at all—of Dana Shelby and Vanessa Patrick. I thought of what each of us is capable of, of what we will do out of necessity and self-preservation and how they can't compare to what we will do for love. I thought of all this and I knew. I knew where Lauren was. I knew who had her. I knew who was behind it.

As quickly as I could I found a phone box and called Collins.

"I need Sam's phone number," I said.

"You mean Detective Smith?"

"Yes," I said. "He went home, right?"

"I have some bad news for you," Collins said, "or haven't you got time for it?"

"The number. Please. It's an emergency."

He covered the receiver with his hand and yelled to someone for the number.

"We found out who bribed the inmates to fight," he

said. "You'll never guess who it was."

"Dana Shelby," I said.

"How the hell did you know that?" he said.

I didn't say anything.

"What's going on? Why do you want Sa—Detective Smith's home number?"

"Things are starting to come together in my mind," I said. "Got a quick question for Smith. If I'm right or I'm not I'll call you back."

"Why did Detective Shelby do it?"

"For love," I said.

"Huh?"

"For a man's great love for a woman. Why else?"

"I don't understand."

"The number. Please. I'll call you back. I promise."

He gave me the number. "Call me right back," he said. "I mean it. Right back."

We hung up. I dropped some more change and dialed Sam.

It took a few minutes but he finally answered. It took a few more minutes but he finally woke up enough to understand who I was and what I wanted.

"Huh?" he said. "Riley, what the hell? I just got to sleep."

"You said Vanessa Patrick was a prostitute, right?"

"Right."

"For who?" I said. "Who does she belong to?"

"The black market guy," he said. "Lee Perkins."

Chapter 31

"I know," I said.

"You know what?"

"Why'd you do it?" I asked.

"Why'd I do what?"

"Did you make just enough to put Gladys in Oak Cove or did you get some money to retire on too?"

Henry Folsom opened his mouth to speak, but nothing came out.

If possible he looked even older now, his face and ears even more oblong, his features even more feeble, his world-weary eyes even more sunken.

"What is thirty pieces of silver with inflation?" I asked.

"I don't care about money," he said. "You know that. Only Gladys. There's nothing I wouldn't do for her. You understand that. I know you do. You don't know how bad it's been, the hell I've been through with her. You don't know because you've been so wrapped up in your own little world you don't know what's going on in the real one. Hell, there's a war going on. People are dying all around us."

"You tried to make me one of them."

He shook his head. "I never did."

The room, the hall, the entire hospital was as quiet as death, only our tense, dry voices piercing the veil of silence.

"How can you say that?"

"What is it exactly you think I did?" he said.

"Why don't you tell me."

"I let the mayor get Gladys a place in Oak Cove."

"Buy her a place," I said. "Buy you."

"I knew what that would mean."

So this was the sound of idols falling down, I thought. The end of mentors and once great men was no different than the end of anything else. Paltry. Pathetic. Kind of quiet. Whimpers not bangs. What a pitiable piece of work a man is.

"That he was buying *you*," I said again.

"No," he said. "Absolutely not. That there might come a time when he'd want me to turn a blind eye to something or do him a small favor. That's all. And that's all I did."

"Guess you and I have different definitions of that word *small*."

"I made a phone call," he said. "I kept my mouth shut. Nothing more."

"A phone call?"

"He calls me middle of the night says he needs a cop in Tallahassee."

"Not just any cop," I said. "A compromised cop like you. A cop for sale."

"I gave him Dana Shelby."

"And it got him killed."

"That's not on me."

"Is Lauren being kidnapped? All of Harry's crimes?

183

De Grasse's dead girls? Is anything? What do you take responsibility for?"

"For doing what I had to for my wife," he said. "And I'd do it again."

"What was Harry Lewis's connection to Lee Perkins?"

"What connects all men like them? Money and power. Black market stuff. It's big business—biggest since hooch during prohibition. You think I care about that? You think I want one dirty dime from their treason? I don't. And I haven't taken any."

"Except the dirty dimes paid to Oak Cove," I said. "Where you think they came from? It's blood money and you know it."

"You wouldn't do the same for Lauren?"

I didn't say anything.

The lack of light in the dim room seemed to have changed somehow, as if shifting shadows had—as if everything had shifted.

"You haven't killed for her and worse? And she's just your girlfriend—actually, another man's wife. Gladys is my everything. Has been for thirty-three years."

"Do you know how many people have died?" I said. "What about De Grasse's victims?"

"A hundred of Harry's whores couldn't come close to my Gladys, but I had nothing to do with any of that. And I tried to arrest Flaxon tonight."

"You tried to kill him to cover up your crimes, but he was faster."

"I . . ."

"Do you know what Perkins is doing to Lauren?"

"I have nothing to do with any of that. I told you.

All I did was call Dana. Nothing else."

"And since I found out Lauren's alive?" I said.

"Nothing. What?"

"Trying to cover your crime. You dropped a dime on me and Clip. Have tried a few times to have us killed. Out on Highway 20, at the Panther Room, the bus station."

"No. That's Perkins. Not me."

"Who told Perkins we were heading to Tallahassee? Who let him know we were going to the Panther Room? At least, you thought we were, but we split up so you only got Shelby."

"I haven't . . . I didn't do any of that. I just . . ."

"You sounded so shocked when I called you after the shoot-out at the bus station diner. You thought I'd be dead. So stop lying. You're more involved, knew more, did more, than you're saying."

He didn't respond.

"Who put Perkins in touch with Burke?"

"You don't think a man like Perkins knows a hundred men like Burke?"

"There's only one man like Burke in this area," I said. "And you put him onto me and De Grasse and—"

"I'm sorry, son," he said. "I really am. I didn't intend any of this. I just . . . I was just doing what I could for my wife, what I had to for the love of my life."

He had been like a father to me. His use of the word *son* reminded me of that. It also triggered something inside me. Shook loose an image—actually several of them. In quick succession I saw my dad, Darryl Collins, Henry Folsom, and Ray Parker. Since Dad's death and Collins's cold control and indifference, I had been searching for a father figure and I had chosen badly. Twice. The hole inside me left by my dad's departure had left me vulnerable and blind and had cost me plenty.

"You ever call me *son* again I think I will have to kill you," I said.

"Jimmy."

I shook my head and turned to leave.

"I'm a good cop," he said. "Think about all the good I've done, all the people I've helped, all the criminals off the streets because of me."

"You were a good cop," I said. "At one time. No more. You were the best. Now, you're a criminal. You've become the very thing you hate. You're compromised, corrupt. You're no different than Harry and Perkins and all the rest."

"What're you gonna do?"

"Get Lauren back," I said. "Or die trying."

I took a few steps, then turned back around.

"Oh, and in case y'all do succeed and kill me, forget what I said earlier about you finding Lauren and taking care of her. She'd be better off dead."

Chapter 32

"You kill 'im on the spot?" Clip asked.

I shook my head.

"Hell's wrong with you?" he asked.

"Take longer than the drive to Tallahassee to tell you."

"You think he callin' Perkins right now tellin' him we on the way?"

"I honestly don't know. Maybe. I don't know. Depends on if he has anything else to cover up, if he thinks we've told anyone or will. I just can't say."

"Could if you'd'a killed 'im," he said. "Dead man can't dial."

I laughed.

"Maybe time to change this shit to the Jones Detective Agency," he said. "Things be simpler I in charge."

"No doubt."

"So we don't know if we walkin' into a ambush," he said.

"Think we have to assume we are."

He nodded. "You gots a plan?"

"Was hoping to come up with one on the drive over."

"Do I need to be quiet and let you . . . ah . . . formulate?"

"Tell me what you'd do," I said.

"First I'd'a killed the old cop," he said.

"For doing what I'm doing?" I said. "Anything for the woman he loves."

"So you the same as him?"

"Haven't found a line I won't cross yet."

"You coulda shot Burke in the back when he was leaving your office," he said. "You coulda snuffed out the little bit of life left in that old cop right there in his hospital bed."

"Yeah," I said. "I'm swell."

"He got bought off by a fuckin' dirty politician," he said. "He been lettin' people get killed to cover it up ever since. He helpin' a black market motherfucker profiting off the death and misery of others—robbing the poor to fatten the rich."

We fell quiet.

I thought about what he had said. Maybe he was right. But even if he was, I understood the impulse behind what Henry had done.

We rode along in silence for a long while, our car the only one on the long, lonely highway.

"Got anything?" he asked eventually.

"Not much, no," I said. "Narrowed it down to a few options."

"Yeah?"

"We go in alone or we go in with backup."

"Wow," he said. "Scary how good you are at this."

"I know."

"Thought you said a few?" he said.

"Couple of different options on the backup," I said, "so I don't count that as just one."

"What they?"

"Get Collins to do a raid," I said. "Or get some private help."

"Such as?"

"How 'bout the fool you knocked out earlier tonight and some of his friends?"

"Turn the negroes loose up in that whites-only joint?" he said, nodding, seeming to relish the idea. "You invite either group to the party—the cops or the negroes—you lose control of the situation. They both trouble. Just be different kinds."

"Was thinking of using them only if we already lost control of the situation . . . as a sort of last resort. Not backup so much as way backup. But you're right, the risk is too great to Lauren."

"You think he got her at the hotel, or somewhere else?"

I shrugged. "No way to know. That's another reason not to involve others."

"Downside is we outgunned and outmanned, just go in and get our asses killed."

Chapter 33

"**Y**ou wake me up twice in one night," Lee Perkins said. "It's unprecedented. I'll give you that."

We were back in the empty Cypress Lounge of the Floridan Hotel on Monroe. He was still in the same silk pajamas, house slippers, and robe.

Though just having been awakened again, though it was nearly dawn, his dark, oiled hair was perfectly in place, his small, dark, dead eyes, wide awake.

"As early as you go to bed," I said, "I'd think you'd be about to get up anyway."

"I go to bed early. What of it. I sleep in. I can afford to. Got nothing to do with you. Like I said, I should have bumped you off for disturbing me the first time—"

"It's not like you haven't tried," I said.

"—and here you are again," he said, finishing his thought with a small smile twitching at the corner of his thin lips.

"Sorry to interrupt."

"Speaking of bumps," he said, "the hell happen to your head? You didn't look so good the first time you woke me up tonight. Now . . . well, now you look a lot worse."

"I'm okay," I said. "About to be great."

"And you won't know when I have you rubbed out," he said, "'cause you'll be dead."

His voice was low and flat, monotone and menacing.

"You know why I'm here," I said. "You know what I want."

"Forty thousand," he said.

"What?"

"I could make a lot more, but you told me that sweet story about you two kids and you showed respect by not coming in with cops and guns and threats. And you left your nigger outside this time. I like that. So, I'll take a loss on my investment and you can have her for forty-thousand."

"Is she here?" I asked. "Can I see her?"

"She is here. If you're worried about her being defiled, she is not—at least no more than she already was. She's still convalescing. Actually, I didn't even add in my expenses related to that. Well, no matter. I'll be a fool for love too. Why not? Seems everybody is these days."

"Can I see her?" I asked.

"Oh, did I forget to answer you on that?" he said. "No, you may not."

"Will you take a check?" I asked.

The amused little smile danced at the corner of his thin lips again. "My business is cash only I'm afraid."

"An IOU then," I said.

"You're beginning to strain my patience, Mr. Riley."

"How much are you worth?" I asked.

Without the slightest hesitation he said, "Four million and change."

I nodded and thought about it.

"A little less with what I pay this guy," he said as Burke walked into the room. "Took you long enough to get here."

"Takes what it takes," Burke said. "I came straight. Soldier," he said, nodding toward me.

"Burke," I said.

He walked over and stood close to where Perkins was sitting.

"So," Perkins said, "we doing business or shall Mr. Burke see you to your car?"

"Would you entertain an offer?"

"Look, I'm a businessman. If the offer's good enough I won't just entertain it, I'll show it the time of its life."

"I'm prepared to offer four million," I said. "And change."

This time there wasn't just the hint of a smile but the full-blown, thin-lipped mean thing itself.

"My life for the girl's," he said. "You'd be way overpaying if you had mine to offer, which you don't. So it is amusing, but that is all."

He stood and turned toward Burke. "I'm going to bed. Take care of this for me, would ya?"

I stood too.

"One more offer," I said.

"Yes?" he said, a weary frown on his face.

"Old-fashioned barter," I said.

"You have nothing I want," he said.

"You sure?"

"What then? Spill. You're quickly becoming tiresome."

"Your sister," I said.

"But you don't have her," he said.

"But we do," Clip said from the open doorway behind them.

They both turned to see Clip holding Doris Perkins in front of him, his gun to her head.

He was holding her just like we had discussed, in the exact spot I had told him.

While I had been talking to Perkins, he had snuck in and up to her room. It was the best plan I could come up with and so far it was working just like I had hoped.

Doris was disheveled and drowsy, maybe even drugged. Above heavy, hooded lids, her hair stood out on the top and left side of her head.

Clip began easing into the room, pushing Doris before him, her slippers shuffling on the floor.

"Pull your guns out slowly and drop them on the floor," Clip said.

"I can take him out," Burke whispered to Perkins.

"Are you certain?" Perkins said.

Burke didn't respond.

"Sorry," Perkins said. "Do it."

"Now," Clip said. "Or I splatter her brains all over that bar right there."

"Okay," Burke said. "Okay."

He began withdrawing his weapon and I knew he intended to shoot Clip, not drop it to the floor.

As he did, I withdrew the small revolver in my waistband at the small of my back, stepped forward, and back-shot both men—Burke first, then Perkins. I squeezed off one round each in the back of each man's head. Dead center in the back of the head.

Two quick pops. Two bodies crumpled to the floor.

Trading my honor, my code, my character for my life, my love, my Lauren.

Neither man died immediately. Both writhed and gurgled a bit, but not for long.

A short, dark-haired man ran in, his gun drawn.

"What's goin'—" he started.

Clip turned and shot him in the face.

Doris had yet to really react.

I stepped over her brother and walked toward her.

"Where is Lauren?" I said.

"What?" she mumbled breathlessly. "Who?"

"Lauren," I said. "Where is Lauren? The girl from the hospital. Where does your brother have Lauren?"

"Lee?" she said.

"Yes. Lee. Where does Lee have Lauren? Take us to her room."

"Pretty Lauren," she said.

"Yes. Pretty Lauren. Where is she?"

"Sick Lauren," she said.

"Where is she?"

"Her room . . . Her room's beside mine," she said.

I took off running.

Chapter 34

Out of the Cypress Lounge.

Gun drawn.

Down the empty hallway.

Alert for more security.

I had been so close to her just a few hours ago when I had gone up to confirm Doris was really here. Right beside her. In the very next room.

Up the staircase.

One flight. Then another.

As I turned to start up the next flight, another one of Perkins's men was there.

He went for his gun. I shot him in the chest before he could unholster it, the rapport deafening in the stairwell, stepped over him, and continued up the stairs.

When I reached Lauren's floor, I opened the door and looked down the hallway.

No one.

Continuing to her room, I tried the door.

It was locked.

I tapped on it two quick times and stepped to the side.

When it opened, the face that appeared in the narrow crack was Armando. I pressed the barrel of the gun to the tip of his nose and said, "Give me your gun."

He did.

"How many inside?"

"Just me."

"Come out."

He opened the door slowly, then stepped out into the hallway, the tip of the gun never leaving the tip of his nose.

As he stepped out I used his body, which was still blocking most of the doorway, to take a quick look inside.

The room was dim and there was one blind spot, but it didn't appear there were any other gunsels inside.

"I thought you didn't even know where his sister was, let alone that he had Lauren."

"I didn't," he said. "I swear it. Not until after you left tonight. He called me in and told me everything and sent me up here to guard her."

"From me?" I said. "You're guarding her from me?"

"I—"

"Over here," I said. "Away from the door."

He stepped over and I shot him in the nose.

A quick clap, a spray of blood on the wall behind him, and he fell to the floor.

I ran into the room and into the barrel of a .45 semi-automatic.

Without hesitating I fired, ducking away from his shot as I did.

Click.

Click.

Two dry fires. I was out.

He wasn't out. He fired two live rounds, but he had ducked out of the way from what he had thought would be my shot, and the movement had caused him to miss.

"You're out," he said, righting himself and aiming down at me.

"Please," I said, holding up my hands.

He laughed. Then his head exploded.

As he fell to the ground, I turned toward the sound of the shot and saw Clip standing there, gun still held out in front of him.

I jumped up and ran over to the bed.

The hotel bed had been removed. In its place, a hospital bed.

And there she was.

My beautiful, perfect girl. Alive.

I began crying immediately. A hard, gut-wrenching sob that seemed to come from somewhere inside me I didn't know existed.

My knees buckled and I went down.

As I pushed myself up, I saw Clip pulling the man's body out of the room and then close the door.

As I stood, Lauren slowly opened her eyes and looked up at me. Then came tears of her own. Unlike mine, quiet, dignified tears that leaked out of the corners of her eyes and trickled down her cheeks.

"Soldier," she said. "I knew you would come for me. I knew it."

Through the window the dawn was breaking, a soft, hopeful, orange-gold glow in the east.

"You found me," she said.

"Yes I did."

"Again."

"Are you okay?" I asked.

"Am now," she said.

"Now and always," I said. "I told you we'd make it."

She nodded. "You did," she said. "And you were right. The long dark night is over."

Chapter 35

"How're you feeling?" I asked. "Really."

"Better," Lauren said.

That was how she always answered.

"You always say that," I said.

"It's always true," she said.

It was the first time we had gotten out. We were back behind the Cove Hotel near the bay. I had pushed her out in a wheelchair and we were sitting near the water. It was a quiet Thursday morning—two days 'til Christmas, and we had the place nearly to ourselves.

The sun was bright, its rays bouncing off the bobbing waves of the bay, the day clear, the breeze brisk, cold but not too cold.

Our last few days had been spent in seclusion, in recuperation and recovery. We were both in bad shape— just how bad I wasn't really sure yet—but we were together and, as she kept saying, getting better.

"You wanna talk about what happened?" I asked.

"I don't need to, but I don't mind," she said. "Honestly, not much. I was a prisoner and they treated me as such—and they let me know horrible things were coming—but mostly I was just treated like a patient. A few of the guards told me what they were going to do to me, but no one actually did anything."

The relief I felt was indescribable.

"All I did was think about you," she said. "About you coming for me. About us being together. I knew I could endure anything, survive anything, as long as that was even a possibility. I didn't know how badly you were hurt or if you had even made it until they began to tell me how they were going to kill you. Then I knew. I knew you were alive. I knew you would figure everything out. I knew you would come for me. I knew we'd be together. I really knew it."

I nodded.

We were quiet a long moment, holding hands, healing, enjoying the bay and the day.

We were staying in a room at the Cove because we had nowhere else to go—no home, no money, no plans, no prospects.

We had nothing but each other. We had everything.

"You shot men in the back for me," she said. "Murdered them."

"I did," I said.

She started to say something but stopped.

"Does it change how you feel about me?" I asked.

"What? No. Not at all. It's just . . . I still can't . . . I just can't believe you did it. How did you do it?"

"It was easy," I said. "It was for you."

"But . . . what about . . . what's that line you're always quoting about—"

"I've changed it a bit," I said. "Yet this inconstancy is such as you too shall adore. I could not be honorable, dear, so much loved I not you more."

Her breath caught and she brought her weak white hand up to her heart.

We were quiet a moment.

"You . . ." she began. "You really love me more than—"

"Anything," I said. "I love you more than anything."

She studied me for a long moment, her eyes searching mine. "You do, don't you?"

"I do."

Tears of pure joy began streaming down her cheeks, streaks of happiness and love and nothing less than the meaning of life.

Tears of my own trickled out of my moist eyes, and we wept in silence for a long while.

A good bit later, she said, "What're you going to do about Henry Folsom?"

"I'm not sure," I said. "Not thinking about him or anything else right now. Only you. Only us. Only this."

"I still can't believe he did what he did," she said. "Then tried to kill you and was going to let them . . . do what they were going to do to me."

I nodded, but didn't say anything, and once again pushed Henry Folsom far from my thoughts.

"What if he had . . . what if they had succeeded?" she said. "What if they had killed you and . . ."

"He didn't. They didn't."

"I regret every second we haven't been together since we met," she said.

"Me too."

"Let's not be apart any more than we absolutely have to ever again," she said. "However long or short that is."

I nodded. "We won't be."

Her words made me wonder if she knew more about her condition, about her prognosis, than she had let on. I had to get her to a doctor to see what we were looking at, what we had to deal with moving forward.

"What about Miki Matsumoto?" she asked. "What will become of her?"

"We'll figure that out too," I said. "We'll help her have . . . as good a life as she can."

"Where is she?"

"The last place her uncle would ever look," I said. "She's staying with Clip."

"I need to thank Clip again," she said.

"You don't think the first thousand times were enough?"

"What he did," she said. "What he has done for you and for me . . ."

"You can thank him some more tomorrow," I said.

"Tomorrow," she said. "I like the sound of that."

I smiled.

"Tomorrow," she said again. "Has a nice ring to it."

I thought of the quote from Macbeth and wondered if it were echoing through her mind too.

""Tomorrow, and tomorrow, and tomorrow, Creeps in this petty pace from day to day, To the last syllable of recorded time, And all our yesterdays have lighted fools, The way to dusty death. Out, out, brief candle! Life's but a walking shadow, a poor player, That struts and frets his hour upon the stage, And then is heard no more. It is a tale, Told by an idiot, full of sound and fury, Signifying nothing.'"

"Tomorrow and tomorrow and tomorrow," she said.

"That means something so different than it might have. If you hadn't found me, hadn't saved me, if we hadn't . . ."

"But we did," I said. "And I did. No out, out, brief candles, us. No tale told by an idiot. No sound and fury signifying nothing."

"No, none of that," she said. "No walking shadows. And all our yesterdays brought us to today, to this day, to be together—today, tomorrow—"

"And," I said, "tomorrow and tomorrow and tomorrow."

And thinking of another line from another great writer, I took her hand in mine and looked out over the bay, from the small boats rocking in the distance to the trees on the shore beyond, and in all the broad expanse of tranquil light they showed to me, I saw the shadow of no parting from her, but one.

About the Author

Multi-award-winning novelist, Michael Lister, is a native Floridian best known for literary suspense thrillers and mysteries.

The Florida Book Review says that "Vintage Michael Lister is poetic prose, exquisitely set scenes, characters who are damaged and faulty," and Michael Koryta says, "If you like crime writing with depth, suspense, and sterling prose, you should be reading Michael Lister," while Publisher's Weekly adds, "Lister's hard-edged prose ranks with the best of contemporary noir fiction."

Michael grew up in North Florida near the Gulf of Mexico and the Apalachicola River in a small town world famous for tupelo honey.

Truly a regional writer, North Florida is his beat.

In the early 90s, Michael became the youngest chaplain within the Florida Department of Corrections. For nearly a decade, he served as a contract, staff, then senior chaplain at three different facilities in the Panhandle of Florida—a unique experience that led to his first novel, 1997's critically acclaimed, POWER IN THE BLOOD. It was the first in a series of popular and celebrated novels featuring ex-cop turned prison chaplain, John Jordan. Of the John Jordan series, Michael Connelly says, "Michael Lister may be the author of the most unique series running in mystery fiction. It crackles with tension and authenticity," while Julia Spencer-Fleming adds, "Michael Lister writes one of the most ambitious and unusual crime fiction series going. See what crime fiction is capable of."

Michael also writes historical hard-boiled thrillers, such as THE BIG GOODBYE, THE BIG BEYOND, and THE BIG HELLO featuring Jimmy "Soldier" Riley, a PI in Panama City during World War II (www.SoldierMysteries.com). Ace Atkins calls the "Soldier" series "tough and violent with snappy dialogue and great atmosphere . . . a suspenseful, romantic and historic ride."

Michael Lister won his first Florida Book Award for his literary novel, DOUBLE EXPOSURE. His second Florida Book Award was for his fifth John Jordan novel BLOOD SACRIFICE.

Michael also writes popular and highly praised columns on film and art and meaning and life that can be found at www.WrittenWordsRemain.com.

His nonfiction books include the "Meaning" series: THE MEANING OF LIFE, MEANING EVERY MOMENT, and THE MEANING OF LIFE IN MOVIES.

Lister's latest literary thrillers include DOUBLE EXPOSURE, THUNDER BEACH, BURNT OFFERINGS, SEPARATION ANXIETY, and A CERTAIN RETRIBUTION.

CPSIA information can be obtained at www.ICGtesting.com
Printed in the USA
BVOW08*0216150916

462217BV00005B/7/P